Disappear, Love

Love-LovePublishing—Madison, WI
Paperback Edition: 978-0-9852015-7-9
Hardcover Edition: 978-1-961823-08-2
eBook Edition: 978-0985201586
Title: *Disappear, Love*
Author: E. Hughes
Available formats: Digital | Paperback | Hardcover

Hardcover Edition release: 2024

Any resemblance to persons living or dead, as well as any location, event, or entity is purely coincidental. This novel is a work of fiction.

Disappear, **Love**

A novel by E. Hughes

(2nd edition)

<u>Other novels and works by E. Hughes:</u>

<u>Fiction:</u>

Sixth Iteration
Disappear, Love
Business as Usual
Infatuation
A Mediterranean Romance: The Capa Royals
The Sapphire Chronicles: Broken Lair
Hello (A Screenplay)
Beyond the Plain (Poetry)
Digital Smiles (Poetry)

<u>Children's Books:</u>

Penelope Helps Mom and Dad
Penelope: Be Kind to Animals
Penelope: Super Duper Spectacular Princess Ballerina
Penelope: Don't be afraid
Penelope Holiday Cheer
Garden of Secrets

<u>Nonfiction</u>
Time and the Multi-Universe: A philosophy of time and time travel
Starting Your First Patio Garden: A Coffee Book
Family in a Time of Covid-19: The Truth about Coronavirus, How to Protect Yourself and Prepare
Reality Unbound (coming soon)

Chapter One

"Why on earth would you cut your hair? You are a hot mess! Sometimes I don't know what to do with you..."

I looked at mother and rolled my eyes. She was at it again... complaining about the way I looked. When I was little I used to wear a Brewers baseball cap to ballet class...Mother would squint her eyes, pout her lips disapprovingly, and tell me to pull my pink tutu over my flat butt..."Can't catch a bee without a stinger," she'd say in that sugar coated voice of hers.

Mother was a perfectionist, which is probably why I'm so messed up.

She stood in my bedroom, hands parked on her slender hips as she examined the condition of my room. She wore her perfectly coiffed dark hair swept into the neatest bun I'd ever seen. She was the perfect housewife...like Mrs. Cleaver, or better, Claire Huxtable but without the legal pedigree.

"Victoria… Are you listening to me?"

"It's not your hair so why are you worried about it?"

Mother sighed. "You look like a boy."

"Good! Maybe people will shut up about me finding a boyfriend and leave me alone for once."

"What kind of man is going to want a skinny, knock-kneed, bald headed girl? You need to marry a nice Dominican boy and start acting like a grown up. Your father and I can't pay your bills forever."

"If you want me to move I'll move."

Mom swung her petite body around my bed, dumped the pillows from out of my pillow cases and tossed them into her laundry basket.

"*You* don't make enough money."

"I'll move in with Dana," I taunted.

"With Dana?" mother asked, turning her head to the side to look directly at me. "I'm starting to wonder about the two of you."

And I was starting to worry about *her*. Mama had the nerve to complain about me living at home but hated the idea of me moving out.

"Wonder what?" I snapped.

I slipped my feet into a pair of tennis shoes and rolled the bottom of my skinny jeans.

"About you and Dana hanging around so

much. The only person you want to be with is *her*. Why don't you find a nice young man and settle down."

"You sound like a broken record."

Mama rolled her eyes as she collected the dirty t-shirts and socks littering the floor.

"Is that all you think about?"

"Somebody has to! It's been a year and a half since the accident, Victoria. It's time to move on."

Mother looked up at me, sadness in her eyes. "I worry about you…that's all."

"I'm twenty-four years old. I can take care of myself, OK?"

"I gave birth to you, honey. I know how old you are!"

I felt like a teenager. Unlike the fully independent trendy hipster I *used* to be before the accident and the year of grueling physical therapy that forever changed my life.

"Ugh. Don't remind me," I groaned.

Mama dropped the dirty linen into a laundry basket and frowned as she picked it up and propped it on her hip.

"Victoria Taisha Lawford? You never answered my question."

"We're not lovers! It's just a stupid haircut. A pixie cut. In fact, it's not short enough to qualify as a *pixie*. I can still put it in a pony tail. Women wear haircuts like mine all the time."

"I spent fifteen years of my life growing your hair out and you go and chop it all off in one swoop! You're so ungrateful."

"Dana said it was cute."

"Who cares what Dana thinks? And what kind of girl runs off and joins the police force anyway? She acts like a boy, too. "

"Normal girls. Like Dana. *Women* like me and Dana. Gawd, you're so old school. Newsflash, mom. It's not the 1950s. Women are a formidable part of the workforce. She joined the police department four years ago. She's a detective now."

Mom rolled her eyes.

"I don't know how you stand her. Her mouth is too big for me."

I grabbed my army jacket and draped an over-sized messenger bag containing my laptop over my shoulders.

"That's why she's my friend and not yours. I'm taking my bike. I'll be back tonight."

Meeting Dana was just the excuse I needed to get out of the house. I would have walked downtown to get away from my mother's irksome old fashioned ways.

"At this hour? And for goodness sake! Can you please keep your room clean? Last time I checked the word *'maid'* wasn't stamped on my forehead. *Does this look like the Hilton to you?"*

"Whatever. Dana's waiting for me. That greasy little diner on 3rd street burned down. The cops think it was another arson job. Say what you want about Dana but at least she's helping me. I'm going downtown to freelance another article for the Journal."

"Well, good luck with that."

Mama shrugged like she was bored and walked out.

I didn't expect her to take an interest in my career anyway. The only thing mother ever cared about was finding a man and keeping him. Never worked a day in her life and refused education beyond high school. Despite this, she was well read. She had to be to hook the kind of man she wanted. By the time she met my father she had already gone through a string of wealthy men. My parents married when she was in her thirties. She had me at forty-three.

The only man mother ever truly loved was my father. He wasn't rich, like the others. He was a struggling real estate agent when they first met. Somehow, he managed to win her heart and they've been happily married ever since. It was the one good thing she'd ever done.

A crackle of thunder made my bedroom window rattle as a burst of rain poured down in sheets. I left the house a few minutes later, hopped on my bike, and pedaled like a maniac all the way downtown. We lived a few beats outside of the city where highway met country road. Our house was the two-story, four-bedroom, country home with the wraparound porch out in the middle of nowhere. It was a half-mile away from the water tower, yards away from a blue windmill in a big grassy field not far from the ancient willow tree overlooking a pond with baby ducks waddling in it. I pedaled as fast as I could down the gravel path from our house until I hit the bike trail leading to Madison Heights, just off road.

I was nervous as I rode my bike out there alone in pitch black darkness. The route I took was like something out of a horror movie. Dilapidated warehouses and abandoned buildings accounted for most of the scenery. But after the accident I vowed I would never drive again. In fact, driving scared me far more than the thought of Freddie Krueger lurking out there in the bushes.

Luckily, I made it to Dana's crime scene forty minutes later, safe and sound. There, fire trucks, squad cars, errant fire hoses, and police officers littered the street.

The wheels of my bike rotated slowly as I pedaled into an area that had been sectioned off by yellow police tape as I looked for my friend Dana.

She was a tall woman, tough with a lean build and crystal clear eyes that sparkled like green ice. She wore her auburn colored shoulder-length hair pulled into a ponytail. I could hear her barking orders as I followed the sound of her booming voice across the street.

The two of us made an odd pair, and it was amazing how we'd managed to stay friends over the years. I was the aimless artsy one; she was focused and professional. It was her drive that led her to make detective in four years. Though some of the guys in her district would suggest she'd been pushed ahead of the pack because she was a woman, so Dana worked hard to prove herself.

"Hey, what we got here?" I asked, far more cheerful than someone entering a crime scene should be. A police officer standing nearby gave me an irritated look.

"Get your ass behind the line, Tai. You're messing up my crime scene," Dana yelled.

Dana was lead arson detective on the arson case. This was the third fire in six weeks…the modus operandi was always the same, mostly restaurants, though occasionally a barn here or there in the middle of nowhere.

I backed off. "What crawled up your ass and died?" I asked.

"Your mother. She called looking for you. I told her I was in the middle of something and she chewed my damn ear off."

"My bad. What's the scoop?"

"Same guy. Same M.O."

Dana grabbed a piece of debris and held it in her hand, smoke still rising from it.

"Looks like he used an accelerant. Probably took less than an hour to burn this place to the ground."

Dana chucked the debris aside. A man wearing a CSI jacket picked it up and placed it in a baggie marked "evidence."

"And how do you know this?"

"Our dog sniffed it out. Judging by the char marks near what used to be a window, I would say the fire burned there first, spreading across the dining area to the kitchen. My forensic team is analyzing paint chips and pieces of wall."

I pulled my notebook out and took notes, wondering why anybody would want to set this place on fire. The diner was just a tiny storefront on a busy two-way street, owned by a sweet hard working old couple. I'd eaten a burger in there once.

"What about the other restaurants? Any chance he'll come back?"

"It's inevitable, Tai. Unless we catch him first. He's picking them off one by one."

I followed Dana to a window where she kicked broken glass into the restaurant and looked inside.

"I'm taking bets. Will it be the Japanese restaurant across the street or The Pancake Shack on 5th?"

"Anything's possible at this point. We'll keep our eyes on both."

I scribbled some more. A uniformed officer gave Dana a chart. She gave it a cursory read, took a pen out of her jacket and signed the document.

"Wanna get some lunch tomorrow?" I asked.

"Let's do that. Across the street?"

I looked up. "Why?"

"I told you I'm keeping an eye on the place. The suspect might come back to have a look at his handy work. They always come back."

"Cool. We'll catch up."

"How'd you get out here?"

"I rode my bike."

"This time of night? I'll give you a ride home. I'll be done in a few minutes."

Dana snapped her fingers and a young officer

with a dog pushed his way through the crowd towards us.

"Nah, I'm good. I'm gonna grab some coffee and hammer away on my laptop for a while."

"You sure? It's raining pretty badly out here."

Thunder crackled again as if to emphasize her point.

"I like rain. I'll catch you tomorrow," I said, hopping on my bike again.

I rode across the street, dodging a fireman as he rolled a large dirty white fire hose back onto a fire truck. He gave me a nasty look and spat on the ground, wiping a smudge of black soot across his cheek with the back of his hand as he dried his mouth.

I continued across the street and parked on the sidewalk in front of Satsuki Japanese restaurant, my back facing its large red sign as I took in the devastation unfolding across the street. The air smelled like barbecued pieces of wood and melted plastic.

Overpowered by the fumes, and realizing my laptop was probably wet, I went into the restaurant to see if I could salvage the damned thing. I sat down, taking a window seat. I did a double-take when I saw my reflection in the glass. My hair looked mangy and wet and mascara ran down my mocha complexioned cheeks leaving a trail of ink colored tears in its wake.

The laptop beeped. I stared at the blank white screen of my word processor and hammered out a title. As I typed, a young Japanese waitress wandered out of the kitchen to my table. The restaurant was empty, the chaos across the street driving customers away for the night.

"Excuse me, may I take your order?" the waitress asked. She held a tiny notebook in her hand.

The woman was young, all of twenty years-old with big pretty eyes and dark hair pulled into two pony tails. She looked liked a school girl.

"I'll have some coffee," I answered.

"I'm sorry. We shut our coffee maker down for the night. We close in an hour. Would you like some tea instead?"

"Tea would be great, thank you."

I looked away, typing again. A few minutes later the young woman returned, setting the tea on the table before me. She stood for a moment, gazing out of the window.

"A shame the rain didn't put the fire out."

I looked up and gazed into her soft pale face.

"It was a nice restaurant," she muttered absently. "You look cold. My brother told me to offer you a blanket. Would you like one?"

"I'm almost dry and the tea is keeping me warm… but thank you."

"I'll be in the kitchen if you need anything."

"Maybe some more tea."

The girl nodded.

Lightening lit the sky, revealing a glittering of stars behind dark ominous clouds. My eyes darted to a silhouette outside the window. A woman in a tan trench coat slipped out of a dark car, closing the door behind her. I watched as she raced into Satsuki, wiping rain water out of her eyes. A few seconds later the door opened and the woman walked inside, an open newspaper covering her damp hair. She took the paper off and shook it, droplets of water falling to the floor.

I drained the liquid in my cup unsweetened, gazing blankly at my computer screen again. Suddenly, a familiar voice called me by name.

"Tai? Is that you?"

I looked up, immediately recognizing the woman.

"Rachel?" I exclaimed. "What are you doing here? How are you? How are the kids?"

I waved her over, wondering what she was doing out so late. She took her wet trench coat off and shook water onto the floor as she sat down, exhausted.

"Damn rain. I fucking hate it."
Rachel's thick brown hair clung to the side of her
chubby cheeks. She blinked water from long
dark lashes as we hugged across the table,
leaning away from my laptop to keep it from
getting wet. A drop of snot tickled out of one of
her nostrils and her hands looked shriveled and
cold.

"I haven't seen you since…"

"The party," she answered dryly, trying to
light the sopping wet cigarette in her hand.

"I didn't know you smoked."

Rachel smiled. "Neither does Richard."

She flicked ashes into a ceramic tray covered
with packets of sugar and salt.

When Rachel and Richard got married everyone
thought they were the perfect couple. Even their
names matched. Rachel dropped out of college
and married Richard before his unit deployed to
Iraq. She was a twenty-five year-old mom of two
kids and as much as she loved them, hated the
life she'd been dealt. Or rather, the life she
chose....

I looked up to find the waitress next to my
table. She set a cup of tea before me and took the
old one away.

"So…what brings you out on this cold wet

night? Shouldn't you be at home reading the kids a bedtime story?"

Rachel spouted a cloud of smoke into the air, pointing her nose dramatically.

"They're not up this late," she answered, fanning a puff of smoke away from my face. "I was out with my old man. I told him to let me out at the diner."

I almost spat tea out of my mouth. "I hope you're talking about Richard."

"Why would I be talking about Richard? If you must know, I'm having an affair," she answered flippantly.

"Why? What happened?"

Rachel gave me a curious smile and pointed her cigarette at my face accusingly.

"Richard bores the hell out of me, that's what happened."

"What about the kids?"

"What are you, my mother now?"

"I'm your friend," I sighed.

Rachel nodded as she drew from the filter of her ciggie again.

"Good…good. I'm glad I ran into you, actually."

"What's up?"

"I slipped out when Richard went to bed, but he must have realized I was gone because he called my cell twenty minutes ago, wondering where I went. I told him to pick me up. He's been acting real suspicious lately. So if you don't mind, I'd like to use you as an excuse."

"As long as I don't have to lie to him…" I started.

It wasn't my style to get involved. I liked Richard. I wasn't down with lying to him about his wife. Rachel took a puff of her cigarette again. I inhaled, drawing second hand smoke into my lungs, unable to meet her unrelenting gaze. She must have known by the look in my eyes that deep down inside, I was judging her.

"Don't worry about it. He trusts me. But enough about my shit. How are *you*?"

"I'm fine. But sometimes, I miss Everett so much I feel like I'm losing my mind."

"I know, sweetie…" Rachel softly replied. "Just remember he'll always be with you."

…And what if I didn't want him to *'always be with me?'* When will it be okay to move on? Maybe I wouldn't feel so bad about the accident if I wasn't always blaming myself. I met Rachel's pitying gaze.

"When I'm alone in the house I see him as clear as day, standing right there in my bedroom. It's scary as hell but I miss him so much I don't want him to leave. I feel so torn. Whenever I think about being with someone else, you know, dating again...I feel like I'm betraying Everett. Like I don't deserve to move on and have a life without him. It feels so wrong..."

"Everett would want you to be happy, Tai. Give it some thought."

"Now you're sounding like *my* mother. I know Richard's boring and all but just thank your lucky stars he came back from the war alive."

Rachel sighed.

"I'm sorry. I must sound like a real bitch when I talk about my husband."

"I wouldn't say that..." *Out loud.*

We looked out the window. A green minivan pulled to the curb, right in front of Satsuki's. The door opened and a man jumped out and slammed the door behind him. He gazed at the burnt out diner across the street, a confused look on his face.

"There's Richard. Just a head's up before I leave..." Rachel said.

I gave her a questioning look and she gestured towards the kitchen.

"You might end up with somebody a lot sooner than you think."

I turned around. The young Japanese waitress

appeared at my table again with the check. *What in the hell was Rachel talking about?*

I looked at the young woman. "Thanks, I'd like to pay my bill now."

She left and I grabbed the second cup of tea and drained it quickly, searing hot liquid scorching my throat. The young woman returned a few minutes later and sat the check on the table. I stayed another twenty minutes and finished my article. When I was done, I paid the bill and left her a small tip.

Thunder rumbled and lightening streaked across the darkened sky. I loved rain, but lightening scared the shit out of me. Especially at night, when I'm alone in bed staring at the ceiling, trying my best to fall asleep. I'd see things in the flickering shadows and angry flashes of light.

I looked back at the restaurant and thought about going inside. But the flashing green "OPEN" sign in the window powered down and a red "CLOSED" sign flickered on. I should have taken Dana up on her offer to drive me home.

I hopped on my bike, swung my bag over my shoulder and pedaled away. I could hear the wheels crunching on top of pavement it was so quiet out, save for the pitter patter of rain on pavement. Everything in Madison Heights shut down at 11:00 pm, the boring little city that it was.

It was lonely out, but I didn't need an mp3 player to keep me company. Nature had already provided an orchestra, like the thundercloud pouring rain on top of my head and the cold merciless wind battering my face. I was grateful when I made it to the deserted little bike path not far from my house nearly an hour later.

I entered the blackness of the bike path. There, pavement gave way to dirt and treacherous shards of rock where the mud had been washed away by the rain. I wasn't intimidated. I knew every crevice, rock, and hill...I could ride the bike path with my eyes closed. But the most ungodly aspect of the ride was the treacherous wind. Branches bent and swayed ominously overhead and my face was cold and red. Discomfort rendered the terrain completely unrecognizable as I blinked rain from my eyes. I just wanted to get home.

I adjusted the messenger bag swinging from my neck. It was getting heavy. I could feel the straps burning into my shoulders. I turned the handles on my bike swirling a full 360 degrees to a screeching halt, the tires kicking mud into the air. My fingers were numb. I blinked water from out of my eyes, wiping them with the back of my hand. I got off the bike and kicked the wheels, knocking mud from between the spokes.

I got on my bike again. Darkness loomed ahead. I realized the worst part of being alone, was the feeling that I *wasn't* alone.

I looked over my shoulder. I saw someone in the distance, about a block away. I wiped my eyes hoping to make out one of my neighbors. Who was this stranger and what was he doing on our path this time of night? He rode a motorbike and moved quickly towards me.

Our house was the only one for about two or three miles and the bike path ended well before then. I squinted, trying to make sense of the shadow, but he was gone. Where was he? He was there only a second before....

I was used to seeing ghosts around the house, but out here?

My thighs burned. Mud was clogging the wheels again and I had only gone a couple of blocks.

The bike path veered left of the road down a steep hill and whenever it rained, water and soot rolled down, washing the path with sludge. My bike sunk into the mess like it was quicksand, when suddenly I hit a bump and lurched forward, the chain on my bike snapping violently.

I was airborne for what seemed like an eternity. Then gravity took hold, ripping me out of the air like a disgruntled old man with a cane. I grunted as I landed face down in the mud, blood dripping down my face. I tried to breathe but my chest hurt. Worse, the impact of my fall broke my laptop, smashing it to pieces.

I laid there a moment mumbling "fuck" and "shit" over and over again in frustration. Every bone in my body ached and the whole world went dark. Water from the puddle in crept into my nose. I coughed, choking as it burned the inside of my nostrils.

Then I heard it. The sound of a branch snapping underfoot.

There I was…alone, defenseless, and immobile in a deserted wooded area with Freddie Krueger. What in the hell was I thinking coming out here like this?

Then I heard it again…another footfall in the brush.

"Who's out there?" I called.

I looked up, a desolate gray sky poured infinite drops of rain onto my face.

I waited quietly for the stranger to make his move as I wiped blood from my bottom lip, tasting dirt and soot…my nostrils leaked like I was a two year-old child with a bad cold.

A thin cloud of cigarette smoke settled overhead before slowly dissipating. The stranger was nearby.

I drew myself to my knees, palms on the ground. The cigarette in the stranger's mouth dropped into the puddle at my finger tips, its dim red light slowly fading away in the darkness. Fiery red embers hissed at death by drowning.

The footfalls drew nearer, surrounding me in every direction.

"I'm just trying to get home," I reasoned, giving the assailant a sideward glance.

I gazed into the darkness, hoping to make something out. A man of average height, lean, if not a bit muscular stood on the other side of my bike. I strained my eyes as I tried to make out his face.

"Do I know you?" I asked.

The man looked at me then reached into his front pocket, hand lingering a moment.

I didn't wait for him to make his move. I scrambled to my feet and took off.

My heart was beating so hard I thought it was going to explode out of my chest as I tripped over fallen branches and stumbled through a bush where I cut myself on a vine of thorns, searing my skin away.

There I was…dodging boulders, evading trees and the possible axe murderer following me. I looked back, but only for a split second. He kneeled over my bike then stood, lifting it out of the mud. I ran like that creepy cop in the Terminator, and soon, saw light at the end of the tunnel. The trail, not far ahead, lead to the highway and the gravelly path to my house.

The sound of the stranger's footsteps beating behind me in the distance soon gave way as I breached light and cut across the field. When I made it to the house I leapt two stairs at a time to the back door and banged it open with my fist.

I slammed it closed behind me. Safe, but exhausted, I slid to the kitchen floor in a heap and sobbed my eyes out...yet quietly, so mother would not hear me.

Chapter Two

The first thing I saw when I opened my eyes the next morning was my cracked laptop. It sat on the nightstand next to my bed, a grim reminder of the night before.

I sat up, a blinding headache nearly pushing me back down. There was a lump on my temple where I apparently hit my head on a rock when I was thrown from my bike. Panic made my heart beat hard against my ribcage. Had I imagined the stranger?

I got out of bed, wearing the pajamas I put on the night before, and limped to the bathroom. I stood before the mirror, inspecting the cuts and bruises on my arms and legs. A tiny plum sat beneath my eye. I looked like I had been in a fight.

I washed up, wiping remnants of grass and dirt from places you couldn't imagine. Then I brushed my teeth and hair then went downstairs to eat breakfast. Mother always cooked a big breakfast. Taking care of the house was her only joy in life. I sighed at the thought of such an existence.

I sat at the kitchen table. Mother stood before the stove scrambling eggs while simultaneously rolling turkey sausages around in a frying pan.

Not a hair on her head was out of place. She wore it in a bun. At eight in the morning, she was fully dressed, makeup already on her face.

She wore a jogging suit most of the time but didn't jog. Mother simply liked the way she looked in her outfits. Dad obviously liked the way she looked too. They couldn't keep their hands off of each other. Sometimes he'd sneak from behind and tickle her sides.

Mother used the spatula to scoop eggs and sausage onto a plate then turned to set it before me, looking down at my face for the first time.

The spatula fell to the kitchen floor.

"Dear lord! Victoria…what happened to your face?" Mother shrieked.

In other words, what kind of man was gonna want a *beat up baldheaded old bumpkin* like me?

"I fell off my bike, mother."

Concern gave way to a look of anger.

"I told you not to ride your bike at night, and in a damned thunderstorm at that."

I ignored her, scooping eggs onto my fork.

Dad walked in, took one look at my face and grabbed the morning paper from the kitchen counter. Mother sat a plate of food and a cup of orange juice before him. He took a sip, flipped the pages of his paper open and began to read.

"How's your story?"

"I'm screwed. I broke my laptop last night."

Dad peeled the corner of his newspaper forward and peered at me from the brim of his glasses.

"You can have the old one downstairs in the den. What are you gonna do about the article?"

"I finished the story but I can't get it because it's on the broken laptop. I'll write it again, I'm just…"

I sighed, throwing my hands in the air. Wasn't like we could really talk with mom in the room.

"What's on your mind, Tai?"

If I told them about last night, they'd freak. Then again, dad was cool…until mom figured out a way to rile him up.

"Nothing. I'm just a little tired…that's all."

"Get some ice on that shiner," he ordered, gesturing towards my black eye.

I got up, went to the refrigerator, grabbed a tray of ice and poured the contents into a plastic zipper bag. I held it against my eye. Mother shook her head in dismay.

"I'm goin' downtown. If you need a ride let me know," dad said.

I sat down, ready to finish my breakfast. Mother laid a hand on my shoulder.

"Victoria! Before I forget to remind you, get your bike off the porch. I nearly broke my neck this morning."

I got up, walked slowly to the back door and looked out. There it was...my bike sat on the porch steps, the back wheel spinning, chain in place.

I went outside in my pajamas and hauled the bike off of the stairs, scanning the yard nervously for my would-be attacker.

Weird things like this happened all the time. When I fell asleep the night before, I opened my eyes in the darkness and for a fleeting moment...saw someone sitting on the window sill. Was I crazy? I parked the bike and went back inside trying to figure out how it ended up on the porch. Maybe dad saw it when he was out for a jog and brought it back.

Satisfied, I went to the den and got my father's old laptop. I remembered some of what I wrote for the article, but wondered if someone else had already beaten me to the story. According to Dana, the department planned to release a statement later that day. I sat at my desk and turned the laptop on.

When the old processor finally booted up, I went into my dampened messenger bag and took my notepad out. The words were smudges of ink running down the pages.

I swore loudly and slammed it on the table. The department was playing the arsons down, calling them "isolated" or "copycat" fires. Madison Heights had a serial arsonist on its hands and the public deserved the truth. But I also had an obligation to the department as its civilian researcher I had to get permission from Dana who was the lead detective on the case *before* I wrote an article alerting the public to the pyromaniac on the loose in our city. It was a matter of choosing my words carefully.

Dad gave me a ride downtown a few hours later. As promised, Dana waited outside of Satsuki, the Japanese restaurant across the street from the burned out diner.

"Thank god you're not on that damned bike," was the first thing out of her mouth.

I took my sunglasses off and put them on top of my head.

"What happened to your face?" Dana exclaimed.

"It's a looong story."

"Well...I wanna hear the story so let's get

inside where you can tell me about it."

I hated when Dana talked like a cop.

"Is this an official interrogation?"

"Maybe."

"You wanna cuff me first?"

"I just might, if you don't get your ass through that door."

She opened the door and I walked ahead like one of her criminals. We sat down, taking a corner table where she could watch the rest of the room and keep an eye on the burnt down diner across the street.

"I've been staking the diner out all morning."

"We're not blowing your cover are we?"

"No. I put two guys out there. They needed a break so it's a good thing we're sitting here. What happened to your face?"

The young waitress from the night before appeared at our table. I was slightly relieved. Since the accident, everyone, including Dana, had been overly protective of me.

"Hi, nice to see you again," the young woman said. The name *Mihoko* was on her name tag. "May I take your order?"

She smiled and I smiled back. Dana rolled her eyes and glared at the bruises on my arms and face. I was stalling and she knew it.

We gave the young woman our orders and

she scribbled it in her notepad.

"Alright, enough's enough. Tell me what happened or I'm filing a report."

"I fell off my bike, it's no big deal."

"Fell off a bike my ass…you look like you fell off a damned cliff."

"I took the bike path to my house. Got caught in a mudslide. The chain on the bike snapped and I fell."

"How'd you get the black eye? What happened to you, Tai?"

I waved my hands in mock surrender.

"Fine…I'll tell you the truth. I took the bike path to my house. The chain snapped, and I fell. I was probably out for about thirty seconds. I woke up, looked around and some guy was standing over me."

"You're shitting me!" she squealed.

"I took one look at him and took off. I don't remember the cuts and bruises. Or how I got them for that matter."

"So you rode your bike into a densely wooded area in the middle of the night and some lunatic tried to grab you? What on earth would possess you to do something so stupid? I told you I would give you a ride."

I rolled my eyes. "I'm tired of people fussing over me…enough's, enough's."

The smell of chicken Teriyaki and rice wafted into my nostrils. I looked up. A young Japanese man stood next to our table with two trays in his hands. I inhaled as he sat the plates before us, long dark hair swaying in front of his eyes. He was tall, with broad permanently slouched shoulders. His face was lean and his body thin but sculpted. He looked up and I recognized him immediately.

Squinting my eyes for a better look, I leaned forward, trying to see past the veil of glossy dark hair.

"O? Is that you…?" I asked.

My eyes slid to the muscular lines of his neck, down to the top of his exposed chest. O's heart hammered visibly through taunt rippling, sticky flesh.

Without moving his head, he looked up with his eyes…taking me in…then finished setting our plates before us.

"Victoria."

It wasn't a question. He knew exactly who I was. He glanced at the bruise under my eye then looked away.

"Can I get you anything else?"

When he spoke his voice was a deep vibrato, his accent more prominent than it used to be. I suspected he'd spent much of the past six years back in Japan.

I fumbled over what I should say next. O and I went to the same high school. I used to tease him about his name. "O" was for "Omelet."

"How are you?" I probed. "How long have you worked here?"

I couldn't take my eyes off of his face. He looked younger than his twenty-five years, but the aura emanating about him, something in his dark exotic eyes made him seem older and wiser than he should be.

O was the last person I ever expected to see again. I was aflutter with disbelief, emotions I'd put away a long time ago pushed to the surface like a volcanic eruption.

In high school, I was fascinated by him. He was the most mysterious person I had ever met. I'd known him since the tenth grade.

Sometimes he would walk me to my locker, arm draped around my shoulder like I was his girl as I teased him with question after question about his mysterious name.

"Why do people call you O, again?"

"Because it's my name."

"Your parents would never call you that."

"What are you, an expert on Japanese names or something?"

"It's not like you can blame me for being curious. I never met a boy with a Japanese name like yours. Just O?"

"Maybe it's not a Japanese name."

"It's not American either."

"I never said it was."

"You never said that it wasn't, actually."

O sighed and pulled me by the waist, drawing me so close that I bounced against his chest.

"Is it *Onion?*"

O smiled.

"My name is whatever you want it to be."

I rolled my eyes, shirking out of his grasp as I opened my locker, still reeling from the tingly effects the imprint of his skin touching mine left behind.

"Is it *O*…as in the name of the city you were born in…like Okazaki?"

O rolled his eyes. "I wasn't born in Okazaki, crazy girl." His voice took a serious tone. "Are you going to senior prom?"

I shrugged. "I don't know. Why?"

O wore his hair short back then. I wanted to run my fingers through his shiny dark mane.

"I'll tell you my name on one condition," he said.

"I don't care about your stupid conditions, but go ahead..."

"I'll tell you my *real* name if you go with *me*," he answered.

"Go where?" I asked, shoving my lunch bag inside my locker.

"To prom."

"Really?" The cutest boy in school was asking me to prom!

"Yeah."

I half-closed the locker and looked at his face, trying to ascertain if he was serious. "So what's your *real* name?"

O leaned against the door. "I'll tell you at prom."

"Are you serious?"

"I'm always serious," he answered.

I drilled the books in my hand with my fingernails as I mulled over O's proposition. I'd known him since the tenth grade. Was he for real?

"If you don't want to go just say so."

I looked down the hall. A gang of O's friends were staring at us. He waved them off.

"No or yes?" he insisted.

O wore a plain white t-shirt and a pair of Levi's. He kept his attire simple and sexy. It didn't take much to make him look good...O would look good in a paper bag.

"Of course I'll go to prom with you, silly..."

I slammed my locker shut.

He smiled, eyes hungry and sexy...his

luscious lips parting and moving towards me. I braced myself, ready to accept the warmth of his lips meshing against mine.

"We'll talk about it later," he whispered, slipping by with only the promise of a kiss.

Damn…

I waited until he was out of sight…then texted all of my friends; *"Goin' 2 prom with O,"* I wrote.

Thirty seconds later, my Blackberry blew up… messages from my five best friends.

"O muh gawd"

"Wtf?"

"Wtf? Do he even speak inglish?"

"Nice!"

"Oooh he iz cute!"

"What colorz are you going 2 wear?" my friend Samantha wrote.

I had no idea so I sent him a text message, asking the same thing. An hour later, I got a response, *"I dunno. Whateva u want 2 wear."*

I forwarded the message to all of my friends.

****

For the first time in my life, mother and I were actually getting along. We bonded over prom dresses and boys as we shopped for hours on end in search of the perfect dress.

I eventually settled on a strapless yellow gown, white tulle over yellow satin with crystal beading around the bust that spiraled down into an a-line crinoline skirt, giving it a subtle but regal look. It had a corset back with a hidden zipper, for a snug fit.

I felt like a princess.

At school, I told O what color I was wearing and made sure he picked a tux with a matching white cummerbund and tie.

He complied, assuring me that he'd gotten the right suit.

A few days later, I opened my locker and found a clear plastic case with a yellow, pink and white corsage inside.

The plastic case sat in my locker on top of a bag of ice with a gift tag on the side that read *"from O."*

I stared it, completely mystified as to how he had gotten it into my locker. How did he know the combination? Did he hold *all the keys* to my heart?

I opened the box, inhaling the beauteous scent of flowers. Then I saw it. Under the satin butterfly wings sat a pearl tennis bracelet. I looked around to see if anyone was watching as I tried it on, then I opened my Blackberry and sent a message to the girls; "Tennis bracelet from

O to go w/my corsage!"

SEND.

A few seconds later I received a litany of responses;

"O-M-G"

"*Wtf?*"

"*awwww I'm gunna cry! I want one*"

"*he iz soooo freakin' cute*"

I took the corsage off and put in my book bag. Later that day, I showed it to mother.

"Victoria…this boy must *really* like you," she smiled.

"We're just friends, mom," I said, revealing the tennis bracelet inside.

Mother gasped when she saw it. She quickly slipped her glasses on to appraise the piece of jewelry.

"Baroque fresh water pearls with a fourteen karat gold clasp."

"That is scary amazing how you're able to do that," I said, rolling my eyes.

Mother laughed.

"Awww…he probably emptied his little piggy bank. This is worth at least a hundred dollars."

Mother wiggled the tiny bracelet in her hand like it was a piece of fish.

I covered my ears, "Mommy! I don't want to know the price, stop it."

"So…what do you guys have planned for prom night?" she asked.

I felt like all the air in the room had been sucked out. I knew what she was thinking and I was absolutely terrible at telling lies. What would mother say about me and O getting a hotel room? She'd kill me! It was no secret to anyone, what most young couples did on prom night, not that O and I was a couple yet…

"We're going to prom then we're going out to eat with friends."

"I want you home at midnight. Got it?"

"What? That's not fair!"

"I don't want you and O getting into any trouble."

"I'm not stupid. I'm eighteen years-old! I'm an adult. Besides, it's not like you can stop me."

Mother sighed. "As long as you're living under my roof you will follow the rules. Got it?"

I groaned impatiently. "Please…? We're going to Lillie Anne's with my friends then to-"

I stopped myself before I blurted anything out.

"The Fairmont?"

I looked at mother and gasped.

"I saw the receipt, Victoria." She curled her lips disapprovingly.

"We're not doing anything, we're just hanging

out. O's not even my boyfriend. We're *just* friends."

Friends with benefits...

"You sure?"

"I wouldn't lie to you, mom."

"Alright. You can stay out but…"

"I promise, I won't get into any trouble."

"Good."

****

On the day of the prom, mother took me to Maryanne's Beauty Spa to have my hair and nails done. The stylist and owner of the shop was her friend. She twisted my long wavy tendrils into a bun and when she was done a nail technician glued crystals like the ones beaded into my dress, onto my fingernails.

The girls and I had our hair and nails done at the same spa.

When mom and I got home, we worked on my makeup together, the way the cosmetician at the upscale department store showed us. I put my dress on and mother zipped it in the back.

I wore the tennis bracelet and the corsage O had given me. Butterflies fluttered about in my stomach. Mother took pictures while dad held the curtains back and stared out the window into the darkness, waiting for O to arrive.

I didn't know what to expect. O wouldn't tell me if he rented a limo or some luxury car. The truth was, he could have shown up in a Pinto and I wouldn't have cared. I just wanted to be with him and the night could not be more perfect.

I sat on the sofa, praying I wouldn't stain my dress as I waited. Prom started at 8:00. It was already 8:15 and O had yet to arrive. Mom was starting to worry.

"He'll be here," I told her, the muscles in my stomach clenching. I resented the way she doubted O. But I also knew my mother well enough to know how much she hated when people were late.

An hour later we were pacing the floor side by side. Where in the hell was he?

Was the ringer on my Blackberry turned off? I checked it again and again. Mother gave me pitiful looks. Seriously, was O going to stand me up?

Text messages from my friends poured in every five minutes.

"Wtf?"

"Where r u?"

"R u and O @ the Fairmont already!?"

"Pls come"

"Prom iz boring w/o u"

I considered, but only for a moment, going to prom without a date...but I needed to hear from O first. Was he in an accident? Why didn't he call? I couldn't enjoy myself without knowing whether or not he was safe.

I sent him a text message. Then I called his house.

No answer. I felt pathetic, and was on the verge of tears but had to put on a brave face in front of mother.

"Are you okay?" she asked.

It was ten-thirty. I rushed to the window, peeled the curtain back and looked out, sighing...prom was all but over now.

I took the corsage off and sat down. "I'm fine. You guys can go to bed. I'm going outside."

I couldn't take my mother's pitying looks anymore.

"You sure?"

"Yes, mother!" I huffed. "Just go to bed. It's embarrassing enough without you looking like that."

"Alright..." mother sighed. "Goodnight, honey."

I kicked my shoes off and walked to the pond on the other side of our property then climbed into the tire swing in my big beautiful yellow and white dress. I didn't care if it got dirty. Prom was almost over now anyway.

I let myself swing back and forth, going higher and higher, then slowing down again as the wind whipped through my hair. The bun I wore loosened, errant tendrils of thick dark locks sweeping my shoulders in long wavy cascades.

I laid my head against the rope, wiping tears from my face. It was quiet, save for the 'cree cree cree,' an orchestra of crickets performing their songs in the night.

I sat under a glittering of stars that lit the sky like a crystal blanket…there was only three weeks of school left before graduation and I would have to see him every day. All I could think about was O, wondering what I would say to him at school on Monday. Then I heard it; a stirring in the brush. I looked up. I thought it was a rabbit at first, until I heard the sound of a branch snapping under foot. I waited for the stranger to appear, and wondered if I should make a run for it until I saw his face. O materialized out of the shadows with a duffle bag in his hand and a book bag strapped to his back.

I slowed down, touching the ground with my toes as I stopped the tire swing. I had nothing to say to him about prom. I had nothing to say to him *ever*.

"Tai..." he called, gently setting his duffle bag on the ground. He strode towards me kicking dirt and stones out of his path.

"Leave me alone! I yelled, as I struggled in vain trying to free myself from that odious tire swing in my clumsy yellow prom dress.

O rushed to my side and held it steady as I stumbled out, hastily pushing it away with my foot.

"Victoria..."

His plea hung in the air like a guilty verdict. "Will you listen to me?"

My little cricket friends chirped noisily in the night. The jury had spoken. I shook my head and tried to walk away, but O grabbed me by the elbow and pulled me back.

"Listen to me!" he barked, eyes pleading. "I have nothing to say to you-" I started, when all of a sudden, O kissed me. I pushed him away at first, but he held tight. One of his hands braced the back of my neck, the other clung to my upper arm for dear life.

I splayed the tips of my fingers across his muscular abs, offering faint resistance as the softness of his mouth wreaked havoc on my hormones.

"Are you done yelling at me now? I'm sorry, Victoria," he whispered breathlessly. "Will you please listen to me? I'm sorry about tonight…"

"Where were you?"

O closed his eyes, as though it pained him too much to answer.

The house dimmed, my parents heading upstairs to bed. We were in perfect darkness, save for the flittering glow of fireflies fluttering about.

"I know you're mad," O whispered against my ear, "Do you forgive me?"

"I need to know what I'm forgiving you for!" I demanded. "Why did you stand me up?"

He kissed me again, smiling…and I realized how happy he was to see me. It was the most emotion I had ever seen from O in the few years we had known each other.

With our fingers still entwined, our lips meshed, hearts together. Whatever happened to him that night, we were safe in each other's arms.

"I don't care about the prom," I said. "But you could have at least called to tell me you weren't coming."

"I couldn't," he explained.

"Why not?"

O sat on the grass and hung his head. I sat beside him.

"You're going to ruin your dress," he said.

"You look pretty."

"Thank you," I answered, trying to maintain a semblance of anger. Why let him off the hook so easily? "It's not like it matters, since I'm not going to the prom anyway."

"I went through a lot to get here, Victoria...I just want you to know that."

"What happened?"

O sighed. "It doesn't matter anymore. The whole night is ruined."

"There's still time to make it up to me."

I plucked a flower from the grass and ripped its petals apart. O took the stem from my hand and tossed it in the pond.

"What are you thinking about?" he asked.

"How quiet and peaceful it is," I answered.

"That's how I feel when I'm with you."

"Quiet?"

"Peaceful," he corrected.

I moved aside. He laid his head on my lap, gazing up at the sky. "I'm sorry," he pleaded, again. "You sure you forgive me?"

"I'm still here, aren't I? I just wish you would tell me what happened...we're supposed to be at prom, having fun," I said.

O sighed. "This isn't fun?"

I plucked another flower and twirled it. O took it out of my hand and stuck it in my hair. A frog popped its head out of the water then plopped back in, splashing noisily.

"What about your promise?" I asked.

"What promise?"

"About your *real* name?"

"I told you I would tell you my name if you went to prom with me."

I dumped a handful of grass onto his face.

"That's so unfair!" I exclaimed. It's not my fault we didn't go to prom!"

"Don't do that, I'm allergic to grass…" he cried.

"Then take your jacket off," I demanded.

O complied and we used it as a blanket.

"You ditched me on prom night to keep your name a secret, you dog."

O laughed and scratched the side of his face, a small hive appearing.

"It's too dangerous to know my name."

"Dangerous for who? You or me?" I asked.

"How long have we known each other?"

"Since the tenth grade!"

"And you still don't know my name?"

"*Huh?* You never told me! Even the teachers call you O."

"We went to the same middle school, and sat in a dozen classes together. You've heard my name a million times. If you don't know it by now, then you don't deserve to know."

"Chicken shit! That name of yours must be truly awful."

"What a culturally insensitive thing to say," he gasped. "What kind of name is Vic-toe-reee-uh anyway?"

O pretended to strangle me. I collapsed onto the grass beside him, laughing, as he pushed my back against the ground and straddled me. "And look at your hair!"

"What's wrong with it?" I queried, blinking wildly.

"It doesn't feel like hair. It feels like I'm touching a cloud."

"That's the silliest thing I've ever heard. Nobody knows what it feels like to touch a cloud."

O laughed. "You never let me touch your hair, that's why I called it a cloud."

"Cumulus? Or stratus?"

"Can I touch your hair?" he asked.

"Of course," I answered, gazing dreamily into his hypnotic brown eyes.

O caressed my face with his fingertips then gently sifted through the thick dark coils of my hair. "It feels soft…and fluffy," he whispered.

"Like a cloud?"

"I've always wanted to do that," he confessed,

coiling a lock around his finger.

"What else do you like about me?"

O stared at my face then, slowly leaned in for a kiss. The hairs on the curve of my neck stood as his hand slipped to my spine, pulling me close.

"Wanna hear a story about a beautiful girl named Victoria?"

"Does it have a happy ending?"

"That's for you to decide," he answered, brushing strands of hair away from my face.

"Sure," I started, but O silenced me, finger crossing my lips.

"A long time ago, there was a husband and wife…they were very much in love, but had no children. So one day they kneeled and prayed for a child. The husband said, 'let it be a masculine child…'" he roared.

I suppressed the urge to laugh. O was clearly making it up as he went along.

"And the mother said, 'if it's a girl, then let her be the most beautiful girl in the world.' The couple's wish was soon granted. The wife became pregnant one day and gave birth…it was a feminine child."

I rolled my eyes, and was about to tell him to shut up when O shushed me again.

"Wait—there's more," he said, clearly enjoying

his story. "Everyone in town wanted to know why the girl was so beautiful, especially the handsome young stranger who wanted to marry her someday. So he hid under her bed one night and spied on the girl, hoping to learn the secrets of her heart. "

"Wow, a handsome stranger? What did he see?"

"That night, when Victoria fell asleep, an angel awakened and descended from the sky."

"Why?" I asked, mimicking an eager child.

"So he could take her to a stream at the top of a mountain…where a waterfall would bathe her in chocolate."

I gasped. "Why would he do something like that?"

"Because you're the sweetest girl in the world," O answered. "When I look at you, I think of chocolate caramel kisses."

All this talk about candy and kisses was making me hungry. I lay on top of his jacket, with O pinning me against the ground, gazing into my eyes. I was grateful for the dense foliage surrounding us, for the privacy the moment engendered.

"When you think of me, you think of clouds and candy kisses? O, that's so sweet," I whispered.

How could I be angry about tonight when *the* most perfect evening in the world, was to spend it with him? I kissed O tenderly and slowly unbuttoned his shirt. He gripped my hands.

"We don't have to do anything," O whispered.

I was eighteen years-old and ready to become a woman. I longed to be close to him. I kissed O again.

"But I want to."

O sighed with relief. "So do I," he whispered, gazing lovingly into my eyes through a curtain of thick dark lashes.

****

O rested on one of his elbows and looked down at my face, the two of us in the moonlight, still basking in the afterglow of making love. For me, it was the first time.

"It wasn't supposed to happen like this," O said, trying to zip the back of my corset as I held it in place. There was a chill in the pre-summer air. He drew me into his arms and held me close.

"It's better than going to the Fairmont like a couple of horny teens on prom night…it's such a cliché," I answered.

"You're so beautiful, I couldn't' help myself. I wanted everything to be right. I was supposed to take you out and show you a good time."

"But you did," I answered, kissing him on the lips again. I raked my fingers through his short dark hair, but he grabbed my hands.

"Victoria…" he whispered, desperation edging his voice.

"What's wrong?"

O shook his head then rested atop my chest, unable to speak.

"Don't shut me out," I pleaded, holding him close to my bosom.

"I'm not."

O wasn't shutting me out, he was shutting completely down. He reached for my hand, interlocking our fingers.

"Let's go in the house," I whispered.

"What about your parents?"

"I'll lock the bedroom door. They never come in anyway."

"*Maybe later*," he said, snuggling behind me with his arms around my waist. Between kisses, and caresses, we eventually fell asleep.

A few hours later the sound of car tires rolling over gravel awakened us from the beautiful dream we shared. I saw a flashing light. I felt O stiffen then push away, gazing down at my face.

"I have to go," he said.

I looked at his watch. It was two in the

morning. We'd been out there for hours.

"Where? Why?" I asked, hoping to get my question out before he disappeared into the night like a wanted criminal.

He turned, looking me in the eyes.

"Victoria, you turned the worst night of my life into a night I will never forget. I love you, okay?"

His eyes reassured me. I nodded.

"I'll explain everything to you later. We'll finish this, I promise."

O jumped to his feet and put his shirt on. I sat up, crumpled yellow prom dress around me as I held the corset bodice in place, less some unknown person parking in our driveway discovered us. Luckily, we were long out of sight, behind the big tree next to the pond.

"O!" I called, again as he grabbed his duffle bag and backpack. He looked back and blew a kiss at me before disappearing into the brush, leaving me to the echo of my own voice in the still of night, calling his name.

Chapter Three

I sat across from Dana, gazing at O like he would disappear on me again as he finished setting the rest of our food and drinks on the table. Feelings of hurt, anger, and humiliation washed over me like a tsunami. After that night, I moped around for weeks, waiting for him to return. I needed answers, and I needed them now.

"How are you?" I probed. "How long have you worked here?"

His eyes swept over my face then over his shoulder at the kitchen. O's eyes still held mysteries in them.

"This is my family's restaurant," he answered. "I have to go now."

What else was there to say? I had already asked too much, apparently. O and I were strangers now. I was just another customer in this restaurant and he was just a cook. Time had a way of changing people and relationships. He probably didn't remember anything about that night. I felt like a fool.

O was just about to turn and walk away when Dana stopped him, waving a hand.

"Excuse me…*Mr. O?*"

"Yes?"

"I spoke to your sister and father about the fire across the street yesterday. They said you were off running an errand for the restaurant. I apologize for not arranging to talk to you about this sooner. I was wondering if you remember seeing anything suspicious?"

"I work in the kitchen. I don't have any windows back there," he answered.

Dana drew a card from out of her pocket and gave it to O.

"Don't hesitate to give me a call if you remember something later. Okay?"

"Of course."

"I would consider having cameras installed outside," Dana continued.

"We'll give it our consideration," he answered, coolly, shrugging her off.

Detecting a hint of resentment in O's voice, Dana smiled. She watched as he strode away, escorting him to the kitchen door with her sharp green eyes.

"That is one strange dude," she mumbled.

"And what in the hell was that all about?"

I shrugged the question off, looking around. Business was picking up as the lunch hour rush settled in.

"What was *what* about?"

The young waitress Mihoko, appeared and set plates on the table behind us. An elderly couple took bowls of noodles. Mihoko looked up at me then quickly turned her eyes away.

"The waiter. Why were you acting like that? You know him?"

"We went to high school together."

"So he's a friend of yours?"

"He used to be."

Dana grabbed the pitcher of ice tea O left on our table and poured it into her glass.

"He did seem a little stand-offish," she said, shrugging her shoulders. "I saw him looking at you from the behind the kitchen counter, right before he brought the food to our tables."

"Really?"

I wondered how many times he actually looked.

Dana stirred her rice and chicken Teriyaki.

"Anyway, back to what we were talking about...so last night you got away from the stalker. Otherwise, you wouldn't be sitting here. That's good...but did he touch you? Or more importantly, did he put any of those bruises on your arms and face?"

"He didn't do anything. He just stood there, smoking a cigarette."

"I'd send one of the guys to have a look around but from what you're telling me it doesn't sound like his actions amount to anything illegal."

"True, but check this out... I left my bike on the trail last night. The tire was busted and the chain was off. But this morning I found it on the back porch...the chain back in place."

"So he fixed your bike?"

"I guess. He even patched the wheel up."

"I honestly don't know what to make of it, Tai."

"Me either. But I feel like the stalker is out there somewhere...*watching* me."

"Don't get all paranoid. I need you to focus. I'm looking for similar arsons across the country but I don't have time to dick around with that stupid eightieth century database at station. I need you working with me on this case. Anything you can find..."

"Is there a psychological profile?"

Dana leaned back and sighed. "White. Male. Age seventeen to twenty-six. A thrill seeker who likes to watch his fires burn. He probably has a strained relationship with his parents; a detached father, or worse, an overprotective mother."

I scribbled notes into a notepad while Dana sipped her tea.

"Waitress! Can I get some more coffee?" A leather clad middle-aged biker called in a gruff voice.

Mihoko balanced two bowls of soup as she passed him by. "Just a moment, please," she answered softly.

A loud clattering noise rang out. The bowls in Mihoko's hands fell, spilling soup all over the floor. The biker gripped Mihoko by the arm and pulled. "I said I want more coffee!"

The young woman shrank back, struggling to escape the man's vice-like grip.

"What'sa guy gotta do to get some coffee around this dump!"

I heard a swift bang and looked around. The kitchen door flung open and a furious O walked out, eyes fixed on the biker's table. He approached, then grabbed Mihoko by the other arm and pulled her away from the man. Was Mihoko O's girlfriend?

"Order something or get out," he said.

Mihoko stepped back. The unruly customer looked at his friend, then back at O.

"Get back in the kitchen and mind your own business, chink!"

"I don't see any chinks here."

He looked around.

"I do see a troublemaking asshole. Read the fucking sign. This is a *Japanese* restaurant," O said. "If you don't like the service, hit the road."

The second biker, a short dark-haired man in his late thirties, looked O up and down.

"Oh yeah? And what are you gonna do about it?"

O took his apron off and dropped it on the back of an empty chair. The two bikers stood, relishing the opportunity to fight, the taller of the two, cracking his knuckles.

Chatter in the restaurant died down as customers sat frozen in their seats, nervously watching the impending showdown. My stomach was in knots.

The hostess, a slender Japanese woman in her fifties hurried over. She wore a red kimono and a white Orchid fashioned in her silver streaked black hair. The tiny woman moved O out of the way.

"We don't want any trouble," the hostess interrupted. "Everything is fine, please have a seat. I can take your order for you."

"I don't want their money. Tell them to get the

fuck out and don't come back," O said.

I looked down for the first time and noticed the firmly gripped machete in O's hand. My stomach lurched. I looked over at Dana.

"Not exactly a people person is he?" she mumbled.

Dana got up and went to the bikers' table, flashing her badge. "I'm detective Dana Cooper with MHPD, I'm gonna have to ask you gentlemen to leave."

She put the badge back inside of her jacket, flashing the holstered gun around her waist.

The tall blond biker looked her up and down, his face turning a shade of red. "We didn't do anything wrong! Fuck this."

"I look like I give a rat's ass? You're not eating here today so pack your stuff and get out."

The biker pushed his chair aside and scooted by.

"You don't have to worry about me coming back to this dump!" he muttered, looking over his shoulder at Dana.

"Good. One less idiot to worry about..." O grumbled.

The hostess shot him a worried look as he stormed back to the kitchen, angrily slamming his fist into the door as he pushed it open.

"I'm sorry," she said, looking around as if to

address the entire restaurant. "My son is very protective of his sister."

I felt an inexplicable sense of relief. Mihoko and O weren't lovers. She stood by the cash register totaling a receipt, oblivious of the commotion as the two bikers stormed out of the restaurant and zoomed away on their motorcycles.

"Please, enjoy your meal," O's mother continued.

Dana sat down again, then waved Mihoko over for the check. "Lunch is on me. That was more excitement than I was looking for today," she grinned, powerful red hair framing her delicate oval face.

The diners went back to their meals and Satsuki was alive with chatter again. It was like the scuffle never happened.

"Well thank you, dear," I answered, still feeling a bit weird about seeing O again. "I'll let you know what I find when I do the research you asked for."

"No probs. Let's go. I'll give you a ride home," Dana offered.

"I'll take a cab."

I needed time to think and absorb what happened today. I said goodbye to Dana and left the restaurant. She followed me out a few minutes later as I stood by the curb waiting to flag a cab down. We waved goodbye a final time as she got into her car and drove away.

The afternoon rush was beginning to die down and not a cab in sight. Fifteen minutes had gone by and I was beginning to wonder if the lack of taxi had anything to do with the diner across the street burning down. There was usually a fleet of them waiting out front. The drivers either dined inside or got coffee there.

The burnt remains of the diner was intense. I brought my arms close to my sides and hugged my upper arms. Summer was almost upon us but the air was unusually chilly for this time of year. Water from last night's rain made trickling sounds as it streamed into a nearby gutter from the street. I gazed into it, listening to the gulping noise the drain made as water sifted through the vents.

I was torn between feelings of anger and happiness at seeing O again. I was happy that he was alive and well, but the fact that he had not come out to say hello to me sooner bothered me. I recalled the hour and a half I spent at their restaurant the night before. When Mihoko was serving my tea she mentioned her "brother." She said he told her to offer me a blanket when I was wet which meant, he cared about me still. How could I be angry at that? He had to recognize me. After all, he knew exactly who I was when I showed up for lunch the next day.

When I saw him at the restaurant for the first time in six years he barely acknowledged me, much less, offered an explanation for what happened to him all those years ago. Were our lives really so different now, six years later?

The truth was, we *were* different people with different lives now. I had no right to feel angry over something that happened when we were kids. I closed my eyes and sighed. I had to let go of the relationship that never was.

The door to the restaurant swung open, slapping me out of my daze. I felt a presence behind me.

"You just missed your cab," O said.

A yellow taxi zoomed by and I swore under my breath.

"I miss a lot of things," I answered.

The words slipped out of my mouth. I looked away, but felt the heat of his piercing gaze on my back.

He kept his head down as he drew smoke from the filter of the cigarette.

"How's your fiancé?"

The bitter edge of his voice stopped me cold, a chill raking down my spine. I pulled the invisible dagger out of my chest and kept my composure, head turned away to hide the wounded look in my eyes.

"Dead," I answered.

The ever unflappable O didn't blink.

He tossed his cigarette on the ground and crushed it into the cement with his boot, smearing ashes onto the sidewalk. I looked away as he hopped onto the little black scooter parked outside of his family's restaurant, tears blurring my eyes. The tiny engine hummed. I heard him sigh. O looked on the verge of saying *something*, but held back. But then, he always looked like he was on the brink of getting something off of his chest.

I saw another taxi coming my way and waved like I was stranded on a deserted island. The green and black checkered cab screeched to the curb in front of me. The driver, sporting a nasty five-o-clock shadow rolled the window down and snarled;

"Where to?"

"County Rd 353," I answered.

He waved me in. I scurried inside, rolled the window up, and slid down in my seat.

O followed the cab with his eyes as we zoomed by.

Across the street, I saw Mihoko standing in front of the burned down restaurant. O's scooter sped up. For a second, it looked like he was following us as rain barreled out of the sky in sheets, battering the ground below.

O wasn't interested in keeping up with anyone from the past so why would he follow me home? I looked out the back window, watching as he faded into the distance.

The cab parked in the driveway of my parent's house fifteen minutes later. It was still wet and rainy out. I paid the driver and got out, covering my head with newspaper as I ran into the house and called for my mother.

No answer. The parentals were gone…probably at dinner or something. I tossed the keys on the dining room table and checked the answering machine for messages. I got one from an editor at the Journal, asking for an update on the arson story.

The house was quiet, so I hummed a tune, hoping to fill the house with noise as I kicked my shoes off and ran upstairs to my bedroom where it was cold, so cold…that I closed my window. I hated being alone. Pipes clanked eerily. Shutters banged open and closed in the wind. Faucets leaked, "plop…plop…plop…"

I sat at my desk, using my father's old laptop

to type my updated arson story as I pieced clues together in search of a pattern that would link the arsons together. As I read through Dana's reports, something on several pages jumped out at me. **Rain**. It was raining outside when the arsonist set the fires. Not just one or two of the fires, but all of them.

The hair on my neck stood on end as a chill crept into my bones. I looked outside. Droplets of rain battered the window, an ominous cacophony as the sound of pebbles touching down on the glass grew louder. I could almost hear the fire cackling. I blinked at the window's reflection. In it I saw the silhouette of a man, setting a storefront restaurant ablaze. I gasped as the apparition morphed into my dead fiancé.

I shut the image out, squeezing my eyes closed. "Stop it!" I shrieked. "Just stop it!"
 I couldn't even work on my case in peace! I was freaking myself out. So I called Jonathan Lewis, to give him an update on my story.

"Anything new? We're printing in a few hours."

Jonathan Lewis was head editor of *Madison Heights Journal.* An excellent writer and investment guru who amassed a fortune on Wall Street before retiring to do what he loves most…working for the paper.

"I talked to Detective Dana Cooper this afternoon. She's head detective on the case. I'll have a story finished for you in a few minutes," I answered in a shaky voice.

"You have my email, right?"

"Yeah, I'll send it shortly."

"Thanks Tai."

I hung up.

An hour later, my report was finished at last. No broken laptops, ribs or ghosts! I emailed the story to Jonathan.

A few minutes later a "new email" notification appeared on my computer screen. There was a message in my inbox.

"Hey" was in the subject line.

I double clicked the email icon.

"What are you doing this weekend?" it read.

The email was from Jonathan Lewis.

I stared at the screen for a second. Couldn't' figure out if this was work related or personal.

I hit the reply button. *"Nothing. What's on the agenda?"*

His reply was instant; *"You."*

I wrote back; "I like the sound of that."

A "new email" icon appeared a minute or so later.

Jonathan: *"Sushi@ Shima's?"*

Me: *"Sushi? Really?"*

Jonathan: *"Please?"*

Me: *"7 o'clock. What about the story?"*

Jonathan; *"Haven't read it yet but I'm sure it's going to be good. See you on Saturday."*

I closed my email and turned the laptop off. Rain slid down the window in one long sheet as the floorboards in the house groaned and the lights flickered.

The phone rang…jarring, and loud. I held my stomach as if to still my rattled nerves. Dana was on the line. Thank goodness.

"You scared the hell out of me," I said.

"My bad. Are you home alone? If you need me to come over and sit with you, I will."

"No, I'm fine," I answered breathlessly.

"You're not seeing things again?" Dana asked, concern edging her voice. She knew how much I detested being in the house alone. The specter of Everett's spirit had often appeared in my room as I tried to sleep. I'd awake in middle of the night in a cold sweat, weeping uncontrollably. Dana said it was a manifestation of my guilt from the accident. Mother thought I needed a good therapist.

"I'm good," I answered. "What's up?"

"I need your help, Tai. I need someone to work undercover for me on the arson case."

"What are you talking about?"

"The cook. I got a funny vibe from him at lunch. I think he knows more about the arsons than he's letting on."

"He did act a bit strangely today," I replied. "But…we do have some unresolved history."

"It's more than that."

"How so?"

"That's where you come in…what I want you to find out. He's not really a suspect at this point, just a person of interest."

"I haven't talked to the man in years," I mumbled nervously. Dana was my best friend but had no idea that O and I were together once.

"You do undercover work for the paper all the time. How is this any different?"

"I just wonder how far undercover you want me to go."

"As far as you need to. He won't suspect anything, especially after the inquisition you gave him today. You're just an old friend from high school looking to reconnect."

"I'm not sure it's a good idea, Dana. There's some history here…"

"That's exactly why I want you to do it. Are you gonna help me or what?"

"Of course," I groaned.

"Excellent. Get in touch with Mr. O and let me know what you find out…no matter how small.

You have no idea what these tiny details add up to sometimes."

"I'll see what I can do. Maybe ride my bike over to Satsuki tomorrow."

"I knew I could count on you," Dana replied. The sound of Dana crunching down on food filtered through the phone line.

"What are you doing?" I asked.

"Eating. I'm at the coroner's office standing over a dead body. Poor guy struck a match and the house blew up. There was a leak coming out of his gas oven."

I imagined Dana standing over the victim with a sub in her hand.

"That's horrible. Where did it happen?"

"Wilson Street."

"I'll have to write something up tomorrow."

"Good. Let me know if you need anything."

We hung up. I got undressed, wondering if Dana had given me just the excuse I needed to see O. Deep down inside, I wanted to. I needed closure.

I imagined Dana putting a wire under my shirt to catch his two-sided confession on tape.

I opened a drawer and grabbed something to sleep in. I found a white cotton gown with long sleeves. I yanked the fold out, almost like I was unfurling a bed sheet and slipped the gown over my head. I pulled the covers back, my heart palpitating as I climbed into bed for what I hoped would be a good night of sleep. But I just couldn't ignore the howling wind and tree branches tapping on my window like gnarled finger tips. Spirit crushing fear anchored down in my gut. I felt like a little girl...scared of the boogey man.

Then I heard it. A disturbance downstairs...I bolted upright, listening closely. That was no boogeyman.

I sprang out of bed and scanned the room for a bat, a knife, or pepper spray...nothing! So I took an old bronze bowling trophy from my book shelf and weighed it in my hands. With a decent enough swing it was heavy enough to knock the intruder unconscious.

I tiptoed down the hall, the floorboards creaking under my foot. I didn't want to end up like one of those stupid girls in one of those ridiculous slasher movies. I thought about going back to my room to call the police. But I had already made it halfway down the hall so I continued to move forward hoping it was just the shutters banging against the windows. I reached into the darkness in search of a light switch. Suddenly, a sharp pain pierced my side. I let out a yelp and spun around, swinging the trophy wildly. The culprit was an open drawer in the buffet. I shoved it closed.

I proceeded downstairs into the darkness below with only the hand railing for support as my foot touched down on the first step. I took deep breaths, trying to modulate the flow of adrenaline in my blood as I made my way down. But my cool, calm, demeanor shattered like glass when a stabbing pain pierced the bottom of my foot. I shrieked in frustration, knees buckling as I tried to not to fall. I bent down and pulled a small red object from my heel and glared at it in utter frustration.

It was one of those damned Monopoly pieces! A little red motel…. The game board token hurt like a shard of glass. I felt like cussing up a storm. I hadn't seen one in years…can't even think of the last time mom and dad bothered to play. We had a Monopoly board somewhere in the den. What was the piece doing all the way up here?

I was losing it, I thought as I made it to the bottom of the stairs safe and sound. I moved sideways to the kitchen, keeping an eye on living room at the same time. If I needed to swing the trophy I could take someone out. I felt confident about that.

I slipped to the side like a ninja and turned the

light on. When the room illuminated, I screamed at the top of my lungs.

Burglars! Cabinets, drawers, the oven door, and the refrigerator were all open. Broken plates were askew on the countertop and strewn all over the floor. I tried not to step on broken ceramic as I backed away.

A loud bang rattled the front windows. I spun around, feeling a sense of terror. Was that the door? *Who* was out there?

Thunder crackled and boomed a response. I heard a loud zap and the electricity powered down. Shit.

Total blackness now. I tried to get my bearings visually, as I made my way to the phone. I picked it up and pressed a green button to activate a dial tone, but the line was dead. Or rather, the line was fine, only the cordless phones we used lacked the backup battery necessary to keep it working when the electricity was out.

I could actually see little particles of darkness in front of my face as lightening shrieked across the sky.

I heard another crash. Something in the living room had fallen to the floor. It sounded like a lamp or a picture frame. I couldn't tell.

I walked backwards as I made my way

towards the stairs, but forgot about the vacuum cleaner mother left in the middle of the corridor. I tripped, stumbling back. But something broke my fall. I gasped as an arm slipped around my waist as if to steady me.

"Victoria?" the voice said.

I screamed again and a hand covered my mouth.

"It's me!" he said.

"What in the hell are you doing here?" I shrieked.

Better, how did he even get into the house?

"I came to see you," O said. "I knocked on the door and nobody answered. Then I heard someone scream so I broke inside to make sure everyone was safe. I couldn't tell from out there. The lights were out."

He stood behind me, his arms still encircling my waist. I felt myself calming down. I wasn't alone anymore.

O looked around, as if trying to see his way through the darkness.

"Something is wrong in this house."

"You think?" I answered sarcastically.

The floorboards groaned and O's grip tightened around me. I heard the sound of water flowing upstairs.

"What's that?" he asked.

"I think the tub is overflowing."

"Stay here. I'll turn it off."

"O, don't leave me."

He moved and I dropped the bronze trophy. It hit my knee on its way down and landed on O's foot.

O let out a sigh of exasperation. I rubbed my bruise as he bent over to pick the trophy up. O took the trophy away, holding it with his other hand.

"I'll take this…you're a walking calamity," he complained.

We walked backwards towards the stairs together. His breath was warm, his face tucked into the side of my neck.

"Is someone in the house?" he asked.

"*Yeah…*YOU!" I retorted.

"Anyone else?"

"Yes."

"Is he dangerous?"

"*Yes.*"

O swallowed nervously. "What have you gotten yourself into?"

"I don't know. The house is haunted."

We reached the top of the stairs and I directed him to the bathroom, following close behind. When we arrived, my bare foot touched a pool of water. The carpet was slippery and wet. I leaned against the wall. O felt his way around, reaching the tub. He turned the water off.

"I don't believe in ghosts," O called into the darkness.

"Your belief, or lack thereof, isn't the issue. The fact is, there's a ghost haunting this house and it happens to be my dead fiancé."

Lightening streaked across the sky, illuminating the house. This allowed me to see O's face, briefly…

"Hmm…" he grunted, disbelieving.

O wore his trademark white t-shirt and jeans. There was a glimmer of mischievousness in his dark seductive eyes. He looked…delectable.

O walked out of the bathroom, his boots splashing water as he moved towards me.

"I think we should get out of here."

"What about my parents? I have to clean this mess."

"You're not safe here."

"Why?"

"The weather station said something about a tornado. This area, you know, lack of buildings and open fields. It's a dangerous combination."

"Oh…"

"What?"

I rolled my eyes and left him near the bath as I ran to my bedroom. O followed. Another bolt of lightning streaked across the sky.

He grabbed my arm and I pulled away, cringing. I heard a loud creaking noise and turned around.

The heavy cherry-wood bookshelf on my wall tipped forward. I fell back, landing on the bed, hands protecting my head. The shelf came to a halt a fraction away from my face. O held it steady as books tumbled forward, landing around us and on both of our heads. I took a knock from an encyclopedia as I leapt to my feet and helped him push the enormous bookshelf back onto the wall. O grabbed my hand and pulled me away. We ran down the hall to the stairs.

"Please be careful, O."

"I'm trying."

He put his arm around my waist and held on as we walked downstairs and eased towards the door in the darkness.

O unlocked the bolt and tried to pull it open, but the door refused to budge.

"What the hell?" he griped.

A tingling sensation crawled up my spine. I peeked over my shoulder as a cold wind whooshed through the house.

"O! Open the damned thing for goodness sake!" I panicked.

He drew back and pulled as if to use every ounce of strength in his body and the door finally swung open. I ran outside and O followed.

Rain poured down on my head and I had forgotten my shoes. O looked about, his eyes stopping at his little black scooter. He grabbed my hand again and I followed. He climbed on first.

"Get on."

"I'm not getting on that thing! It's raining and I don't have a helmet!" I shouted over the noisy the downpour, hands parked on my hips.

"You won't have a head if you stay in there."

I sighed and climbed on the back of O's bike, leery of riding in the rain. But the scooter was incapable of speeds exceeding 35 miles an hour, so I decided to trust O's judgment and go along with him for the ride.

"Where are we going?"

He didn't answer.

The little bike puttered quietly along the gravel path onto the highway. I wrapped my arms around O and closed my eyes, rain streaming down my face.

The back wheel slipped a few times, turning us askew. I tightened my arms around his waist and gripped his shirt with my hands, trembling.

"Calm down. You're gonna throw us off."

I did what O asked. The last thing I needed was another tragedy.

We arrived at a five story high downtown Madison Heights apartment building. O parked his bike and chained it near the front entrance. I remained on the back of his seat. He gestured for me to spin my legs around and I complied.

"…What are you doing?"

He slid an arm under my legs, lifting me off the scooter.

"Put me down, O! This is so embarrassing."

"You don't have any shoes on. You can't walk around like that out here."

The pavement was littered with spit and other debris, like any typical downtown city street.

I grimaced, showing my disgust as I allowed O to carry me into the building. When we got inside he set me down. Thankfully, the floors were clean. We took a freight elevator to the fourth floor.

It was late and the building was eerie and quiet. O shook water from his hair and wiped rain from his face with the bottom of his white t-shirt. He gave an exasperated sigh, then turned and looked at me; he shook his head, smiling like I was crazy.

I had a zillion questions, but refrained from

asking him anything. *Maybe O will even tell me his real name.* I was optimistic.

He looked at me; starting at my feet then climbing up to my face with his eyes like a chubby eight year-old eyeing a banana sundae.

I was suddenly all too aware of the fact that I wore next to nothing. He could see straight through my wet cotton nightie. Perky nipples sat upright.

"Is this where you live?"

He didn't answer.

The elevator doors opened. I looked around. There were five apartments on each side. I followed him down the hall to his apartment door.

Apartment 404:

We walked inside. The first thing I noticed was the fire escape outside of the windows.

There was a beige sofa, a two seat dining table, and a tiny kitchen with fancy pots, pans, and extremely sharp knives. I stood behind him as he scanned the room with his eyes, in search of something.

Water dripped from our bodies onto the floor. O went into the bathroom and came back out with a towel.

He tossed it at me and I caught it, drying my face, arms, and legs. He stripped out of his wet t-shirt.

I took a step forward and looked around. The room we were in was all there was to see in O's apartment. It was a very big room, with an adjoining bathroom, kitchenette and walk-in closet.

I looked at the scant amount of pictures on his wall and a degree certificate from a culinary school mounted with push pins. My eyes widened. Surely that would have his name on it. But a picture had been placed on the bottom half of it, cascading left to another picture.

Was there no end to his secrecy?

He looked at me and smiled.

"I don't believe in ghosts. But I do believe there's something wrong at your parent's house. Is it like that all the time?"

"Yeah. But mostly when I'm alone. My parents think I'm crazy. You're the first person to experience it with me. It's creepy and I'm terrified of lightening."

He lit a cigarette.

"Hmm…"

Then lowered the blinds. As I watched him I tried not to look at his chest or the muscular lines down his back. Damn. *He must work out all the time.*

O inhaled, blowing a ring of smoke out of his mouth. Then he stared at the floor as if deep in thought.

"A little more than a year and a half ago, I was in a car accident. My fiancé died a week before the wedding. I was driving. I don't think he'll ever forgive me. He won't let me move on without him."

"Was your fiancé an unforgiving man?"

"No. He was a good person. He deserves to be here. Me? I'm not so sure about."

My eyes dropped.

"If your fiancé was a good man, he wouldn't want you to be miserable without him. He'd want you to be happy."

"Then why is he in our house?"

"I don't know. The energy in that place is intense. But I don't think it's your fiancé."

"You think I'm crazy, don't you?"

O dumped his cigarette into an ash tray then flipped a mattress from out of the sofa bed.

"Why were you at my house tonight?"

"I came to see you."

"Well obviously…" I answered.

"I couldn't talk to you at the restaurant."

"Why?"

He shook his head. *The walls were up again.*

"I tried talking to you the other night. After

we closed the restaurant I rode my bike to your house. I saw you on the bike trail. I called your name but you ran away."

"That was *you*?"

"Who did you think it was? *A ghost*?"

"Don't patronize me, O. You don't know how it feels to lose someone close to you."

"I know every bit about how it feels," he answered bitterly.

O strode across the room and stood before me.

"I don't want to hurt you," he said. "But your fiancé's ghost isn't following you around. You're accident prone and tonight was just another one of your mishaps."

"I knew you were going to say that."

O caressed my cheek with the back of his hand, trailing his fingers up to the dark bruise under my eye. I moved it away, the back of my hand pushing into his open palm.

"You never answered my question," I said, changing the subject. "Why were you at my house tonight?"

"Because we have unfinished business."

O left me standing by the kitchenette to ponder his answer. He went to the bathroom and came out a few seconds later, looking me up and down as he walked back in.

"Where were you the past six years?"

O sighed. "Why do you ask me so many questions?"

I shrugged.

"Sit down."

I looked around. The only place to sit was on O's sofa bed.

"I'm still wet."

"So am I."

O walked to the closet and pulled out a white button down shirt. He tossed it on the bed. "Take everything off and put this on."

"There's not much to take off."

He smiled, a thoughtful look in his eyes.

"Can I pour you some tea?"

"Yes. Please."

"This tea is very calming," he assured me.

O went to the kitchenette, filled a kettle with water, and sat it on the stove. He turned the knob and blue flames shot out.

"You have a gas stove."

"I'm a chef. I don't cook on electric ovens."

"Do you like working at your family's restaurant?"

"It's an obligation. I teach a class at the university a few times a week in the summer and work for a company in Europe the rest of the year. What are you doing with your life, Victoria?"

I sat with my legs curled underneath me.

"I'm a civilian researcher by day, writer by night."

"What do you write?"

"*Everything*...but nothing new or literary at the moment. I'm writing articles for the Journal about the arsons."

O stole a glimpse at me from the corner of his eyes.

"What do you know about it?"

"Well...I know the arsons occur at least three weeks apart."

"How do you know this?"

"I looked at the dates of each fire."

"Hmm..."

The kettle whistled and my heart jumped. I was still on pins and needles after the craziness at my parent's house.

O turned the fire off and poured our tea.

My teeth were chattering when he gave it to me. I took a few sips of the piping hot liquid and a calming sensation moved through my body. O took the cup out of my hand and sat it on a nearby table, his fingers lingering over mine. I stared at our hands as he sat beside me. Close enough to reach out and move the fabric of my gown away, exposing one of my shoulders. He kissed it, then kissed the side of my neck, his mouth grazing my cheek, and finally my lips.

Suddenly, I was on my feet, racing to the door. I opened it then ran down the hall to the nearest exit, taking the stairs all the way down to the bottom floor. I heard O calling my name but didn't look back.

I ran outside in the rain then stood, waiting, trying to figure out what I was running from. Was it O? Or was it the promise of being hurt again? I heard my name and turned around. O ran out behind me, white freshly changed t-shirt, soaked and clinging to his dampened skin as rain barreled out of the sky in sheets onto our heads.

"What are you scared of? What are you running from?" he yelled.

"You!" I spat, shouting over the noisy downpour.

O shook his head. "I'm not *your ghost*, Victoria."

"You sure disappeared like one…"

O pressed my open palm against his chest, eyes unwavering as they gazed into mine.

"Not in here," he answered calmly.

We kissed again. A deluge of memories flooded my consciousness as the unspoken emotions we once felt came rushing back. I closed my eyes, longing for more of O's touch. He drew me into his arms, my legs encircling his waist as he carried me into the building again. I could feel the steady rhythm of his breath against my ear. A trail of water dripped noisily onto the tiled floor as he led me back to the elevator in his arms. There, a woman waited, climbing aboard. She pressed the button for the fifth floor and O pressed the button for the fourth, backing me against the panel hard.

The elevator stopped at the second floor.

"I'll take the stairs," the woman muttered, scurrying off.

The doors closed, assuring us of much needed privacy as we gave in to our most fervent desires. O's hands slid under my gown, my backside resting against his open palms as the elevator doors slid open again a few moments later. I locked my legs around him as he carried us to his apartment door and kicked it ajar.

Lightening streaked across the sky and a dimly lit lamp in O's apartment flickered before the electricity powered off. He threw me on the bed, undaunted now, pulling the soaking wet gown I wore over my head in one sweep. There was a chill in the air but I was warm from head to toe. O took his t-shirt off and dropped it on the floor next to my gown. He slid into bed, his lean muscular body climbing on top of mine as he pulled me against him.

"I missed you so much, Victoria. It tore me apart to stay away from you."

"You said you were coming back."

He buried his head into curve of my neck, his lips caressing my skin.

"I know."

"Why didn't you? I waited for you and…"

"I'm sorry," O answered, gazing into my eyes again.

He drew me to him, his lips capturing mine. I moaned softly as his other hand advanced to my inner thigh, the other drawing up and down my spine. My body trembled under his electric touch.

"I still love you," he confessed. "No one but you."

We kissed, unable to restrain ourselves any longer, our bodies colliding in a fevered passion I thought we'd left behind us years ago. Soon, tense, hot flesh poured into mine. The night had taken an unexpected turn. The last person in the world I expected to be with was O, on a sofa bed in a seedy kitchenette apartment, making wild passionate love to the man I was supposed to be *investigating*.

****

I opened my eyes a spell later. O was still asleep, his arms wound tightly around me. I looked around. The lights in O's apartment were dull and the paint on the walls was chipped and old. Nevertheless, the apartment served its purpose. There was a place to shower, eat, and sleep. This was the O I knew...pragmatic. He liked to keep things simple.

The palm of his hand lay open on my breasts.

"Is this the unfinished business you were talking about?" I whispered.

He pulled me into the nook of his arms and squeezed...then planted a wet kiss on my cheek.

"We'll talk about that later."

I waited for Everett to appear in the darkness... his disapproving face glowering down at me for disrespecting memories of our love. O spooned against my backside, and I sunk into the comfort of his arms. And for a moment, however brief, I felt safe again.

Chapter Four

The next morning I opened my eyes to sun rays beaming through an open window, and on the other side, a fire escape where my white nightie had been hung over the balcony to dry. I stretched and yawned deeply as I sat up, drawing a bed sheet around my body. It only took a few seconds to remember where I was, who I was with, and for memories of our passionate night to come flooding back.

A fork scraped the inside of a pan and the smell of eggs filled my nostrils.

O stood in front of the stove making omelets. He turned the fire off and scooped the food out of the skillet with a spatula…setting it on a plate. He was shirtless, wearing only a pair of jeans. He walked to the bed and sat beside me, pulling me in for a kiss.

"Good morning…you slept hard. You know what time it is?"

"Rough night," I answered, blushing. I looked for a clock and found one on the nightstand. It was 9:36 in the morning.

O gestured towards the plate of food and I shook my head.

"I can't stay."

I slipped into the white button-down shirt O had given me and climbed out of bed.

"You can't go out there in that," he answered. "I'll hook you up with something."

"I agree. Definitely not suitable for the ride home…you got a phone book?"

O grabbed a tank top and a pair of slippers from out of the closet and put them on.

"I'll get one from the manager's office. Stay here. I'll be right back."

I sat down and O walked out, the door slamming shut behind him. I quickly scanned O's apartment for any information I could take back to Dana. I jumped out of bed and tip toed across the room, looking but not touching anything until I found a stack of mail on O's coffee table.

I grabbed the envelopes and sifted through each, one by one. The first was a piece of junk mail addressed to apartment "404" or current resident. The second was an advertisement, addressed to the "shopper." I put that one at the bottom of a stack ready to read another when the doorknob turned. I tossed O's mail back on the table again and made myself look busy, plucking imaginary grime from under my fingernails.

He walked inside, big yellow phone book in hand. He dropped it on top of the letters.

"That was fast," I said, trying to hide the disappointment in my voice.

The sound of water running in the bathroom distracted O before got the chance to respond.

"The tub…" O looked at me, confused. "Are you taking a bath? It's overflowing."

I didn't remember turning the water on.

"I'll let the water out."

I skittered by him and went inside, closing the door behind me. I looked at the tub, overflowing with water though not enough to spill on the floor. Everett's face gazed back at me in the ripples. I closed my eyes, shutting him out as I dipped my arm inside and unplugged the stopper. Water inside of the tub slowly drained out.

I heard a tap on the door. I spun around. O stuck his head inside.

"Is everything okay? I thought you were taking a bath?"

"I changed my mind. Do you mind?" I gestured for him to close the door. O complied, smiling rakishly as he backed out.

I stood before the mirror and gazed at my reflection. The swelling under my eye had gone down but there was still a bruise and my hair was wild. I raked it down with my fingers. There was something feral and sexy about the way it looked.

I opened the medicine cabinet and nosed around. There was rubbing alcohol. Shaving cream. A toothbrush…and a bottle of prescription pills. *Eureka.* His name would surely be on the label of whatever it was.

"Are you okay in there?" O called.

"I'm fine…just washing up!" I answered. "Do you have a towel?"

I turned the bottle around and read the label. *Xanax!* Then I followed the small print down another line and saw that the anti-depressant was prescribed to Mihoko, O's sister. Her last name was obscured by a yellow sticker that read "eat with food."

The doorknob turned and O stuck his head inside. I spun around, leaning against the sink with both hands behind my back. Imagine how embarrassing this would be if I were sitting on the toilet!

He gave me a bright blue bath towel.

"Thank you," I answered sweetly.

He closed the door behind him.

I let out a growl of frustration and scanned the rest of the bathroom for another clue. But my efforts soon proved unsuccessful so I gave up and took a shower. A few minutes later, I stepped out of the bathroom, feeling refreshed.

O sat on the bed, cutting a pair of old jeans. He was surprisingly lanky, at 6'0 and I was certain the pants were too long for me at 5'4.

"Try this on."

He tossed them at me.

"What if I wear the shirt and the nightie together?"

O sighed. "It's not enough."

I slid into the cutoffs. He took an old cord and looped it around my waist, using it as a makeshift belt.

"O! I look like a hot mess."

He laughed and pulled me into bed.

"You're beautiful to me no matter what you wear."

We exchanged pecks on the lips, growing uncomfortably comfortable with staying in bed. All of a sudden, O sat upright, pushing me aside.

He rolled out of bed.

"What's wrong?"

"I have class in an hour."

He grabbed the phone and waved me over.

I called a cab. We stood by the kitchenette and hugged.

"You don't have any shoes."

"I'm using my hooves today."

He smiled and kissed me on the forehead. "Wait here."

O went to the closet and came back with four white socks.

He dropped to his knee and layered a pair on both feet.

I looked down at the misshapen cutoffs, the oversized shirt, and layer of socks.

"I think you missed your calling as a stylist."

O laughed, "Whatever, funny ass."

He took me by the hand and escorted me out of the building. The cab was already outside, waiting for me.

"Will you be okay at your parent's house?"

I nodded, kissing him on the lips.

I said goodbye to O and rode home in silence. Everything looked different...and new. For the first time, in a long time, I was happy.

Chapter Five

"WE were *worried* sick about you! Where the hell have you been?" mother shouted, looking like she was at the end of her rope.

My father picked up the phone. "I'll call the search party off."

I groaned, slapping a hand over my face. *Are you kidding me?*

"I'm twenty-four years old. Why on earth would you need a search party? This is getting damned ridiculous now."

Father turned and glared at me, eyes bloodshot red. "*¡Estoy muy enojado, usted soy una muchacha irresponsable!*" he raged.

Dad had a habit of lapsing into Spanish when he was mad, a sample of his hot Dominican blood. Mother pushed him aside.

"The hallway's flooded. There were books all over the damned floor in your room. Broken plates all over the kitchen and you were missing. What are we supposed to think?"

"I told you *before*."

"*Hija*, don't give me that haunted house crap. I don't want to hear it," dad said. "I've had enough."

"I was in my room. I heard a loud crash so I went downstairs. The kitchen was trashed, there were all kinds of spooky things going on in the house! I was terrified so I left. What was I supposed to do?"

"Your dad lost his car keys. He went through all the kitchen cabinets and drawers. We were late for dinner and planned to put everything back when we got home. I left a note on television telling you to close the window downstairs in the den. You didn't. A raccoon got in and ransacked the kitchen shelves. There's no ghost, Victoria."

"The bookshelf in my room nearly killed me. How do you explain that?"

"I told you last week I had to drill a few nails in the shelf because I took it apart, remember?" dad said. "You don't listen. I put the trophy there to weigh it down. When you moved it, the bookshelf fell."

Mother gestured for me to sit on the couch, looking me up and down.

"*Are you on drugs?*"

"Of course not! I'm not stupid, and I am not a child, so don't insult me," I scoffed.

"Your father and I have been talking. We want you to see a therapist again."

"A therapist! For what? I don't need a therapist or your advice, I can take care of myself. If you want me to move, I'll move out. In fact, I'll pack my bags and leave now."

"You need help, Victoria," mother gently interrupted.

"Help with what?"

"We suspect, post traumatic stress disorder or OCD."

"Obsessive compulsive? I am the most disorganized person on the face of the planet. How can I be obsessive compulsive?"

Father sat beside me. "You have a habit of turning the bath water on and flooding the bathroom when you're scared or anxious."

"It wasn't *me!* I'm telling you there's something in this house!"

"I know because I've seen you," dad said. "You don't realize you're doing it."

Gone away were my feelings of euphoria, or thoughts of O. First they accuse me of being crazy, then they accuse me of flooding the house? I inhaled, reigning my emotions in.

"Go to Mercer hospital, Friday at two-thirty to see Dr. Shuter. He comes highly recommended. He runs a clinic in the psychiatric ward."

"So now I'm crazy?"

Father gave mother a pen. She scribbled the address down on a scrap of paper and gave it to me.

"Fine," I griped, snatching the note out of her hand.

I left mother and father on the sofa and went upstairs to my bedroom. The books had been cleared from the floor and placed back on the shelves. The carpet out in the hallway was moist but most of the excess water had been cleaned up.

Was I really responsible for all of this? Had I imagined the fiasco last night? The ghost? The chills running up my spine? *Was I really crazy?*

I showered and changed out of the clothes O had given me. I probably looked like I had been doing drugs when I walked in, no wonder why my parents went berserk when they saw me. It was time to look for a place of my own…maybe in the city, close to all of the action. Close to O.

The phone rang.

Dana was on the line. I sat down, propped my feet high, and started painting my toenails.

"Where were you?"

"Out," I answered, bracing myself for words with Dana.

"Your parents called. I told them you were having a 'Tai' moment."

I stopped at the third toe. "What's that supposed to mean?"

"Nothing. Where'd you go?"

"I spent the night with O."

I heard an intake of breath. I continued polishing my fourth toenail.

"Did you find anything?"

"Not yet."

"You might want to tell us when you decide to do shit like this, Tai."

"I trust O."

I painted another toenail.

"Trust him all you want. I don't know the man so I trust him about as far as I can spit."

"He's a good guy, Dana...I thought someone had broken into the house last night or maybe there was a ghost or something...O showed up. I left, and we spent the night at his place."

"That's all fine and dandy, just don't let it affect your ability to do the job."

"Have I ever? I'll deliver the evidence and you can piece it together. I personally, don't think he started the fires, but maybe he knows something. Time will tell."

I grabbed a magazine and fanned my toenails dry. I could almost hear her blood boiling.

"You're so fucking whimsical," Dana groaned. "Out of the clear blue sky he randomly shows up at your house after six long years?"

"It wasn't random. He showed up on purpose."

"*No shit*...Just promise me you'll watch your back and whatever you do, don't compromise my investigation. I'm trusting you."

"I'm not dumb. I know what I'm getting into."

"Alright, I'll take your word for it. In case you were wondering...which I doubt given all the fun you're having, there was another fire last night."

I sat the magazine on my bed. "Really? I guess that proves me right."

"How's that?"

"It means O didn't do it. He was with me."

"Unless you glued your eyes to his face all night it doesn't prove anything, missy. Besides...the place isn't exactly all that far away from where he lives."

"Let me guess..." I started.

"The Pancake House. The place went up in flames after midnight. We got a dead body so I'm turning the case over to the homicide unit."

"This is horrible. So the arsonist is a murderer now. Who's the victim?"

"A sixty eight year-old man was found dead at the scene. Cause of death appears to be smoke inhalation and burn trauma."

"This has gotten really scary, Dana."

I didn't tell her about the other coincidence,

the fact that it was raining when the arsonist started the other fires.

"I know. To think this guy is out there somewhere waiting to burn something else."

"Did he leave any evidence behind?"

"He managed to leave a few items. And I got forensic results on the tests we ran on the diner the other day."

"What did you find?"

"Traces of a highly combustible liquid, a phenol distillate. Could be an insurance job."

"Thanks for the head's up, Dana. I'll get started on this now."

"Don't put anything about the chemical in your story."

"Right. Don't want the killer to know you're closing in."

"I'm heading back to the scene in an hour. Wanna tag along?"

"Sure, I'll get dressed. See you in a bit."

I ended my phone call with Dana and opened my laptop. I used a national research database to find similar arsons around the country in the past ten years and did some other research I thought would be useful to the department.

When I was done, I wrote an update piece for the Journal and emailed it to Lewis.

I got a reply a few minutes later.

A "new message" notification appeared on my screen.

Sender:

Jonny.Lewis@thejournal4x9.com;

Subject: Re

Body;

"Change of plans. Going out of town. We'll meet three weeks from this Saturday. Is that okay?"

I stared at the screen. The date I made with Jonathan had totally slipped my mind.

I wrote him back;

"See you then."

SEND.

I closed the laptop, grabbed my shoes then went downstairs to get my bike. Mother wandered into the kitchen as I was heading out. She opened the refrigerator and grabbed the orange juice.

"Chasing another story?" she asked, pouring a glass.

I sighed, not in the mood to talk to her just yet. "Yeah. I'll see you tonight," I answered.

I stepped out and closed the door behind me. I rode my bike downtown to the Pancake House, which was only two blocks away from Satsuki, where O helped out at his family's restaurant. I was worried about O. Maybe the arsonist would strike again and he would be the next victim.

The thought of it sent a shiver down my spine. I was more determined than ever to help Dana solve the case.

I met Dana in front of the restaurant an hour later. She wasn't alone. Two investigators stood outside of the burnt out Pancake House, surveying the damages.

Dana, looking more stylish than usual, wore an olive green pants suit and an expensive pair of eyeglasses.

"You're looking sharp," I observed.

Dana smiled.

"You're looking pretty damned smart yourself. You're glowing *and* walking funny."

I played it cool… "If you're lucky, that tall drink of water with the Fireman badge will blow *your* back out too."

We laughed all the way to the entrance where the two guys waited for us. Dana stepped into the group first then waved me over.

"Tai, this is Daniel Wercke, our Fire Chief. He's helping me close my end of the investigation."

Daniel was tall, very sharp looking, and cute, which explained why Dana went out of her way to look good that day. He had thick sun-kissed blonde hair, a lean body, and a cosmetically enhanced set of teeth in his mouth. Probably spent half of his life in a dentist chair. My eyes involuntarily searched his ring finger. Yeah, I could see Dana slobbering all over him.

But she kept her cool, maintaining a professional air.

"This is Detective Omar Wells, lead homicide detective."

I shook his hand. Omar was small for a police officer, bookish, with deep-set intelligent eyes. He wore an afro and a pair of rectangular shaped eyeglasses. He was all of fifty years-old and there was definitely a ring on his finger.

"Victoria Lawford is a freelance investigative reporter for Madison Heights Journal. She's also a part-time research specialist for Madison Heights Police Division."

"Nice to meet you, call me Tai. I scrubbed the national news database for similar fires around the country and found a string of unsolved arsons in Toledo, Ohio three years ago. No dead bodies, just a lot of insurance claims and burned down restaurants. The same phenol distillate was used in each fire. I talked to detectives in the area, they've got nothing."

"Very similar to our guy," Dana added.

"Let's review the physical evidence inside and see what we can come up with."

Daniel opened the burned out door frame, his

hand sliding to the groove in Dana's back. We walked inside as a group.

The Pancake House was just a hole in a wall, now. The smell of burned rubble and debris clung to the air like sweat to a pig's backside.

"There's one more thing," I said.

The group turned to look at me.

"I noticed the fires are not only three weeks apart but it was raining outside when all of the fires were set."

Dana looked like a light bulb had turned on in her head.

"I hadn't thought about that," Dana said. "And it makes sense. Nobody's standing around in the rain. No witnesses."

"Let's keep an eye on the Japanese restaurant down the street. I have feeling they're next on the list," Omar suggested.

My foot crunched down on top of melted plastic, burnt wood, and black soot. I coughed. A layer of ash coated the back of my throat.

The fire chief pointed areas out on the wall where the fire was most intense. He collected scraps of pottery where a plant used to be and put them in an airtight jar. Dana and Omar took notes.

Then I saw it. Something gleamed in the distance. Drawn towards the object, I moved across the room away from the group.

It was a hair comb with ivory and jade designs embroidered into it. I squatted, opening my purse as I took my camera out, snapping a picture of it. When I finished I turned to the others and waved them over.

"What'd you find?" Daniel asked.

"A jade comb," I answered.

"There's nothing on it," Omar said.

I gave Dana a questioning look then followed their eyes to the scorch marks on the wall.

"The comb was left here after the fire. Otherwise we'd find soot and ash all over it," Dana explained. "This was left here after the dust settled. Literally."

"The scorch marks rise all the way to the ceiling. Which means the flames burned the hottest in this location. I believe this is where the fire was started," Daniel continued.

The scars looked like Rorschach blots. Dana kneeled, brushing soot and debris aside with her hand, wearing a pair of latex gloves.

"The accelerant was poured across the floor in this area. We have a char pattern from the window, spilling towards the table and chairs."

She pointed upward. "There's a vent overhead, like the other restaurants."

"What does that mean?" I asked.

"You need three things to get a fire going. Oxygen, an accelerant, and something to initiate combustion…our arsonist was fully aware that starting the fire under a vent would provide enough ventilation and oxygen for the fire to breathe. If you could get some pictures of the place before the arson…." Daniel said.

"Sure," Dana replied. "I'll talk to the restaurant manager about it."

"The manager was killed in the fire," Omar said. The family identified his remains early this morning.

"So the manager's your dead body? For fuck's sake…" she groaned.

Dana took her camera out and snapped pictures of the comb and the ceiling.

"Whoever left the comb is trying to cover their tracks. Let's focus on this area," Omar said.

Omar used an ink pen to lift some of the debris. He then took a plastic baggie from out of his pocket, and scooped pieces of rubble inside.

"Let's send it to forensic. If we're lucky we'll get some DNA from the comb. Maybe hair or left over skin cells if we're lucky," Dana suggested.

Detective Omar scooped the hair comb into another baggie using the tip of his pen again.

"Judging by the comb, I'm guessing the arsonist is probably female," I said.

"I doubt it," Dana replied. "Doesn't fit the profile."

"The arsonist never hurt or murdered anyone before so why would he do it now? We may have a copycat on our hands," Omar replied. "He didn't case restaurant before he started the fire, which resulted in the death of an innocent bystander."

Omar held a baggie full of evidence towards a blown out window, viewing it in the light.

"We'll find out if it's the same person when the toxicology report comes back," Daniel said.

The group walked through the rest of the restaurant like we were touring a museum, pointing out glaring inconsistencies and other evidence of arson. We finished about an hour later then stood outside, contemplating where we should go out for lunch. There wasn't a restaurant left in the area that we could go to, except Satsuki.

I stood silent as the others debated. No one noticed the car parking into a space across the street from where we stood. I watched as the occupant slowly rolled the tinted window down, staring in our direction. I stepped forward and gazed into the darkly-lit cabin.

The young man inside of the car was O. I wondered what he was doing at The Pancake House.

I left the others and walked to the car to greet

him. He saw me and got out, a cigarette dangling from the corner of his mouth. O leaned against the sleek silver colored vehicle, one leg crossed in front of the other.

"What are you doing here?"

He looked over my shoulder, like he was trying to see into restaurant.

"I figured you'd show up eventually. You're helping with the investigation right? Did you find anything?"

O shoved both hands into his pocket like he was hiding something. He wore a white v-neck t-shirt, jeans, and a dark colored European jacket. He smelled fresh, like jasmine-scented soap.

"I'm not allowed to talk about the case. I'm not even sure I'll be helping them out after today, unless Omar needs me."

"Why?"

"It's not an arson investigation anymore. It's a homicide."

O looked stunned for a moment then quickly composed himself. "Someone died?"

"The manager. He was asleep when the fire started. He died of smoke inhalation and burn trauma."

O clenched his fists. "You gotta be kidding me?"

The heel of his shoe kicked the side of the car in frustration.

"What's wrong?" I asked, rubbing his arm supportively. "Are you worried about your family's restaurant?"

He looked up, eyes searching my face. "We're the only one left."

"The police are keeping an eye on Satsuki. Don't worry. We collected a ton of evidence. We'll make an arrest soon enough."

"What did they find?"

"I'm not allowed to say. We were just heading to lunch. You want to go with us?"

O shook his head.

"I thought about you all day today," he said, caressing my face.

"I've been thinking about you too."

"Thinking about what?"

O held my gaze as he drew from the filter again then flicked the cigarette into the street, blowing smoke out the corner of his mouth as he took my hand in his.

"Let's go for a drive. We need to talk," he said.

A gentle breeze lifted the stench of wet, mildew rotted floorboards from the inside of the restaurant and carried it outside.

I looked over my shoulder at Dana. She stared back at us, then at the cigarette O threw on the ground.

I gave her the signal, indicating that I was

about to leave with O. She whispered something to Omar and Daniel. A few seconds later they waved goodbye, leaving for lunch without me.

"What do you want to talk about?"

"Our relationship...I need to know where we're going with this?" O said.

"With what? You don't think it's a bit early to start *defining* our relationship?"

He gave me a cool smile. Probably wasn't expecting me to say that. O slouched, leaning forward as he drew me into his arms.

"We've been at this a long time, Victoria. It's not too soon for anything."

"We haven't seen each other in six years."

"We saw each other last night. *All night*," he teased, smiling.

I rubbed the hair at the back of my neck, nervously. "I know last night happened, but..."

He was still a *person of interest* in Dana's investigation.

O gave me a frustrated look then walked around to the other side of the car and opened the door.

"Get in."

"Where are we going?"

I sat in O's sleek silver-colored car, a sporty looking coupe.

"Are you hungry?" he asked.

"A little."

O walked around to the driver's side of the car and climbed in, stealing a peek at the restaurant as we drove off.

"We can go to your family's restaurant," I suggested.

O glimpsed at me from the side of his eye, shaking his head. "I don't want you at my restaurant again."

My head nearly snapped off of my neck and rolled onto the sidewalk. I turned to look at him, stunned.

"*Why?*" I gasped.

"Just don't go there again. You trust me, don't you?"

"Of course."

He drove with one hand and held mine with the other.

"I need an answer, O."

I neglected the scenery outside as O sped down the road to his apartment. The glow of street signs streaked by like Christmas lights.

I wanted O to slow down but the rush of adrenaline flowing through my body scattered my thoughts like newspaper in the wind. My hands shook and it felt like my heart rate tripled.

The sound of metal shrieking across gravel and tires peeling squealed in my ears. I saw a flash of the accident in my mind all over again. Vomit pushed to the top of my throat. Then we came to a halt. I unlocked the door with jittery hands. The burst of activity made me feel better. The car no longer in motion, I felt oriented again.

O climbed out of the car and walked around to the passenger side.

"Wait here," he said.

He went into the building without me, looking over his shoulder as he went inside. I waited until he was out of sight then opened the glove compartment in search of title and registration. That would surely have his name on it.

The adrenaline in my body surged like I'd eaten ten pixie sticks. I rummaged through the glove compartment where I found a packet of vehicle information.

The packet contained the manual to a stereo system and an operating manual for the coupe.

A folded yellow sheet of paper sat on top. I knew going through his belongings was wrong but it wasn't like he'd tell me his name voluntarily... I gave up on that a long time ago.

I read the first few lines of O's paperwork, gleaning information from the page until I reached the Registrant's name, which read, "Satsuki Japanese Restaurant."

Damn! I folded the sheet of yellow paper and

stuffed it back into the packet. O used the car to deliver food so the car had been registered to the restaurant, probably as a tax write-off.

I closed the glove compartment and nearly jumped out of my flesh. Startled, I looked up from what I was doing. O knocked on the window.

I sighed in relief as he opened the door and gestured for me to get out.

"What were you doing?" he asked.

Had O figured out that I'd been up to something? Or was he always this paranoid?

"I was fixing my makeup," I answered, climbing out of the car.

O stared at my face. "I don't see any makeup."

"That's because you interrupted me."

He took my hand and led me to the apartment building. We stopped by the manager's office to pick up a package and took it to the fourth floor.

"Spices and herbs from overseas," O said, unlocking the door to his apartment, a look of excitement on his face. "I'll cook for you," he said. He took his jacket off and tossed it on a nearby chair.

"Why can't I go to your family's restaurant?

You can tell me anything," I pleaded. "I won't get upset."

"But you're already upset."

I touched his arm. He ignored me and grabbed a pan from an overhead rack and sat it on the stove.

"Of course. I feel like you're hiding me. Are you ashamed to be seen with me?"

O sighed, sucking air through his teeth in frustration.

"No one in my family knows who you are and I plan to keep it that way…for your protection."

I was even more confused now.

"Why would I need protection? Please, tell me the truth O. I won't judge you…I promise."

What were they? Members of the Yakuza?

I tried to force O to look me in the eyes, sliding between him and the stove.

"You're going to get yourself burned," he said, moving me out of the way.

O dropped buckwheat noodles into a boiling pot of water.

"I'll take my chances," I answered.

It was time for the truth. I wanted to know what was going on. Why was he acting so intense?

O brushed past me and opened the refrigerator.

He grabbed a plate of vegetables and sat them on the table. Then he focused…chopping them with a large knife before putting the veggies in a pan and sautéing the ingredients in olive oil.

I watched, impressed by his chopping skills.

"You took a chance on me before and I hurt you. I don't want to do that to you again."

"I don't care," I answered.

He turned and scowled at me. "Why not? You should care."

This was the conversation he wanted to have about our relationship? I was five seconds from walking out the door.

"And you're telling me now? You should have told me all of this *before* I spent the night."

"Things were different last night."

"So what exactly changed between this morning and five o' clock?"

The apartment was just as we left it that morning. Sofa bed out, sheets in disarray and the potted plant in the window withering from lack of water…My gown and the rest of O's linen still hung on the fire escape, billowing in the wind.

O walked over to the sofa bed and sat down.

"The amount of time I have left to spend with you changed."

"You're not leaving again, are you?"

The lump in my throat dropped like a stone into the center of my chest.

O waved me over, patting a spot on the bed, beside him. I sat facing him, on the verge of tears. *Why do the people I care about always leave?*

"I don't know what the future holds, but I

want to spend as much time with you as I can before everything changes."

He held my face in the palm of his hands and kissed me.

I opened my eyes, staring into his. "I love you," he said.

"Seriously, O. Why won't you tell me your real name?"

O sighed as though I had overlooked something of utmost importance.

"What's more important to you, Victoria? Knowing a man's name? Or knowing what's in his heart?"

O left me sitting on the bed. He went to the stove to finish working on the meal he started and I went to the bathroom and sat on the edge of the tub like that *thinking man* sculpture in Paris.

I listened to the sound of water splashing as the tub filled with crystal clear water. The rush of adrenaline still surging through my body from the car ride to O's apartment began to wane. I was physically and emotionally spent. He took so much out of me.

I wanted to be with O even though deep in my heart I knew something about him was amiss. Was it the investigation?

Maybe my feelings for O prevented me from

seeing the truth, despite the ominous warning he gave about hurting me, despite the circumstantial evidence mounting against him in the arson investigation.

I left my seat on the edge of the tub and opened the bathroom door, sticking my head out first. O was on the phone. So I slipped back into the bathroom and listened with the door cracked open. He spoke in a hushed voice to the person on the other end of the line.

"It's too late, Mihoko. It's only a matter of time before they figure it out. "

O looked over his shoulder to see if I was listening, then said something in Japanese and abruptly ended the conversation with his sister.

I recomposed myself then left the bathroom... masking my suspicion with a smile.

"Is everything okay?" I asked.

"Now that you're here..."

O sat our plates on a table near the kitchenette then gestured for me to sit down. He made fish rolled in seaweed, with rice, black beans, and red potatoes. The garnish on the side was Shiso. He designed the gourmet meal to look like a piece of art. The noodles he cooked earlier had been set aside in a bowl for later. I devoured the food before trying a cup of Sake. Then we scraped our plates and washed them in the sink.

It was all very routine, like we had done this a million times before when in reality, it was only our second night together.

O took his shirt off and dressed the bed. I helped, folding the sheet on the other side and tucking it into the sofa as he flipped it over. We sat down and turned the television on. My body pulsed with the desire to make love as I sidled close to him, and snuggled into the nook of his arms.

O pulled my feet onto his lap and took my shoes off. We watched television. O hated everything he saw on TV, even the news…. But I was a reality show junkie. I could sit on the couch like a potato and watch TV all day.
I laid down. O settled behind me and I soon fell asleep in his arms. But everything he told me that night, still lay heavy on my heart.

The next day, we drove to my parent's house and gathered some clothes. I spent the next two weeks much the same…at O's apartment eating, sleeping, and making love.

Chapter Six

"YAKUZA!"** I screamed, bolting upright, hand clutching my heart like it was about to explode out of my chest.

The sound of a canon booming and a series of gunshots shattered the night's quiet. O sat up, blinking his eyes as he looked around the room. He had a calm about him like he was used to the noise as a shower of light rained from the sky.

"What in the hell are you talking about – *Yakuza?*"

Someone banged on the door and I threw O in front of me like a bullet proof shield.

"That's not the Yakuza, silly woman," O groaned.

He sat up, his chiseled physique distinguishable, even in the darkness. Shaking his frustration, he cupped my chin, *"Are you alright?"*

Before I could answer, a voice called through the door....

"Mr. O, we need to get in," a woman said.

O stood and buttoned his pants as he walked

to the door. He peeked through the peep hole before he opened it. A bleach blonde woman of sixty years stood on the other side with rollers in her hair and a frown on her face. She peeked into the apartment nosily, a big rubbery mole on the center of her chin, like a witch.

"You promised me there wouldn't be any trouble here."

O rubbed his eyes. "I'm sorry…but what are you talking about?"

"Do you have the water on?"

I sat up, drawing the sheet around my body. O walked to the bathroom. His feet splashed into a pool of water on the floor.

The culprit was an overflowing bathtub. He turned the water off.

"I'm sorry. I must have left the water on."

The woman stuck her head in the door and looked at me.

"Well, no wonder! Gallivanting around with this fresh young turnip. You young people are so irresponsible! You better hope there's no water damage."

"I'll take care of it, Mrs. Weitzel."

"You better."

O closed the door. He went to the bathroom and cleaned the spill with a pile of extra fluffy bath towels.

I heard another boom. Outside, a series of fireworks exploded mid-air.

"O! What in the hell *is* that?"

O came out of the bathroom and glared at me, a hand on his forehead like he was stressed out.

"It's just fireworks going off at the Fest. What made you think there were Yakuza here?"

I had forgotten all about Taste Fest. The fireworks ceremony was always the night before the parade at the pier.

"A few weeks ago, you said you were trying to protect me. I thought, like maybe, you were involved in something…"

O gave me an incredulous look. "With the Japanese mafia? We have our share of family problems but nothing quite that glamorous."

O opened the window then hopped out, landing on the fire escape. I followed, the bed sheet around me, billowing wildly in the updraft as I scrambled onto the tiny steel grates. O sat on the stairs and lit a smoke, watching the fireworks display.

"Get back inside," he said.

I rolled my eyes. "Don't tell me where to go," I pouted.

O gave me a rakish smile, as if doing his best to get on my nerves. He pulled me into his arms. I stood between his legs, sheet draped around my body roman-style as sparkly festival lights danced across the sky.

"I love you," I whispered, draping my arms around his neck.

O stood, backed me against the railing and kissed me hard. I prayed I wouldn't go falling over the edge as the wind whipped my hair into a state. The side of the building where the fire escape was situated was especially drafty. I looked over my shoulder and shuddered in fear of the dizzying height.

"I love you too," he answered, smothering my face with kisses.

Below, a group of hooligans heading home from the fireworks display whooped and hollered up at us.

"WHOOO YAH MAN! *Tap that ass!*"

A young woman with the group stopped to vomit in a garbage can while one of the young men hurled empty beer cans at passing cars.

"See?" O said. "That's why I told you to go inside. And you thought I was being a jerk."

"If I thought you were capable of being a jerk I wouldn't be here."

O hugged me then let me go, climbing back into the window. He stuck his arm out and I gripped his hand, allowing him to help me back inside.

The next morning I awoke to the cantankerous drill of a marching band. Its trumpet, followed by snares and a set of drums so loud, I thought Zeus had come off of Mount Olympus to play a set on top of a thundercloud. It was too early, and the room was so bright I felt like bitch-slapping the sun.

"What in the hell?" I griped, throwing the covers back.

I shook O out of his sleep. He slept with a pillow covering his head. I climbed out of bed and opened the window, blinding sunlight beaming into my eyes. Outside, a large bumble bee float drifted by with a "Honey Bee Tea" banner draped across its chest.

"O! Wake up," I shrieked. "The Taste Fest already started. What time is it?"

O opened his eyes and read the digital watch on his arm. "It's 12:30," he fussed. "Come back to bed."

He sat up, eyes and face groggy as he pulled me beside him and rolled on top, kissing me on the lips…

"To hell with Taste Fest."

"Why?"

"Too many people."

He rolled out of bed. I gathered the bed sheet around my naked body.

"O! I've been hanging out at your apartment for two weeks and we haven't even been on a date!"

"Would you feel better if I took you somewhere?"

"What do you think?" I said, giving him my best "no shit" look.

"I'll go. But when we come back I get to have what I want."

I climbed out of bed and stood in front of O, hands propped on my hips. "And what exactly *do you* want?"

I eyed him suspiciously.

O cupped my chin and kissed me on the forehead. "To treat you like the princess you are, oh beautiful one."

He bowed mockingly in a gesture of worship, lifting his arms up and down again as he retreated to the bathroom.

"That's not funny!" I said.

"It's not meant to be," O mumbled, motorized toothbrush spinning away in his mouth.

"You don't have to go," I called.

"Really!" O exclaimed, in a sarcastic tone.

He tossed his toothbrush on the sink and walked out.

"Why are you being so sarcastic? I already said you don't have to go if you don't want to."

"Like I need your permission…"

"Now you're being mean."

He looked at my pouting face.

"I'm just giving you a hard time, don't get mad, okay?"

O wrapped his arm around my shoulders, pulling me into an embrace as he gazed into my bewildered face.

"I can't tell if you're serious, sometimes."

"I don't care about the formalities, Victoria, whether we've been on ten dates or none.

All I care about is the end result."

"And what's the end result?"

"Do I have to spell everything out for you? You're so naïve, sometimes."

Now I **was** mad. *"How am I naïve?"*

I put my hands on my hips, curling my lips angrily. Was he trying to piss me off on purpose? I wondered what was going through that head of his. If I didn't find him so irresistible….

"You know how I felt about you, back then, right?"

He broached the subject as though it were taboo to even speak of it.

"We liked *each other.*"

"I didn't like you, I *loved* you. But I was young, I didn't know how to say it or express it to you at the time. When I left, you found someone else, moved in with him, and got engaged...that's a little fucked up. How would you feel if I did that to you?"

"That's exactly what you did to me, for all I know...."

Now we were getting to the crux of it. O opened a cabinet and grabbed a towel, wrapping it around his waist. I stood there gaping at him, unsure of what to say.

"And how would you feel if I left without saying goodbye? Was I supposed to sit around and wait for you?"

O leveled me with a look, slammed the cabinet closed and walked towards me, his eyes clouded with anger.

"That's exactly what you were supposed to do," he snapped. "But I guess it all makes sense," he ranted, gaze sweeping across my face... "because you 'liked' me and that was it."

O had no idea of the agony I suffered after he disappeared. The endless nights I spent, wondering if he was safe, or if I would ever hear from him again.

"That's not fair! I care about you, O. I loved you, too."

"That's not what you said a few minutes ago. But hey, at least I know where I stand," he spat, lifting his arms in utter exasperation.

"I meant every word."

"Don't patronize me," he shot back. "You have no idea…what I had to put up with to be with you."

"What do you mean?"

"Never mind," he said, waving me off.

I gave a sigh of resignation and scanned the room for my belongings. A pile of clothes and my handbag cluttered a chair in the corner of the room. I found it amazing how we'd managed to live in each other's mess the past two weeks.

"Maybe I should leave," I answered quietly.

"I don't want to argue about this anymore," O sighed. "The point I was trying to make is that we found each other again."

He grabbed my arm and pulled me into an embrace, kissing my forehead. I stood completely frozen, totally confused.

"I don't mean to sound bitter. I'm sorry," he said.

With my head pressed against his chest, I sighed with quiet relief. All it took was one touch, one look into his eyes for my resolve wither. He kissed me on the lips. O was alive, and in my arms again. Fighting about the past and who left who was a pointless exercise.

"Fine," I answered, pointing my nose in the air.

"Good we'll leave the past where it belongs."

O kissed me on the lips again. "Are we made up now?"

I broke into a smile and he smiled back. *"For now,"* I warned. "Just don't let it happen again."

"I won't."

His smile was reassuring.

I wondered about O being jealous of my relationship with Everett. We met six months after O disappeared and fell in love. When did O come back? What did he know about us? And how?

"This is weird…never had a naked argument before."

O pulled me into the bathroom. "Have you ever had a naked shower?"

"I think so," I smiled.

****

After the shower we left the apartment and went downstairs to watch the parade. I wore a pair of O's jogging pants and a t-shirt, tying the top over my belly the way I wore them when I was in college. He wore jeans, a t-shirt, and a vest. He looked like a musician.

Taste Fest was a parade where restaurants from all over the state met on Patrol Boulevard to showcase food and other specialties. It was a week-long event with thousands of visitors swarming the sidewalks, booths, and tents for hours.

We joined the crowd that gathered in the street. Vendors at different booths offered up treats and other delicious samples and I wanted to taste them all; fried bananas, alligator sandwiches (yuk!), BBQ Turkey, fried ice cream, caramel pecan cupcakes. O strode behind me catching my hand as he tried to keep pace, but our fingers slipped as I chased a cart selling garlic roasted corn on the cob. I paid a dollar fifty and took a bite, standing on my toes as I tried to see past a portly looking man and his equally obese wife. When I finally turned around, that's when I realized O was missing.

I scanned the crowd for his face. Pedestrians swarmed the streets in packs looking for new and unusual delicacies to sample. Some sat on curbs and watched the floats while others grilled nearby, selling their homemade goods.

The fest was a mesh of exotic aromas.

The crush of thousands of made it feel like it was a billion degrees outside. Thirsty, and hot, I waved to an old man sporting a mustache so thick I thought he was going to suffocate. He pushed a well stocked cooler filled with ice cream, bottled water, and snow for flavored ice cups. I bought bottled water. He looked at me, smiling with mismatched teeth, some off white, some gold…and I don't mean the kind of gold you wear.

"Can I get you anything else?" the man asked, in a thick Mediterranean accent.

Can I get you a toothbrush? But thought better of it. "Maybe later," I smiled.

I bade the stranger goodbye, catching a glimpse of O in the distance, about a half block ahead. I made a start in his direction when a bearded old man in a sweaty t-shirt blocked my path, waving glow necklaces in front of my face. Maneuvering around him, I thwarted the attempted sales pitch and pushed my way through the crowd in search of O.

The Taste Fest covered a mile of Patrol Boulevard. I walked another two blocks east, certain he had gone in that direction.

The fest diverged onto side streets where more booths offered up goods. These were businesses that paid less money than the ones on the Patrol Boulevard. I wondered if he'd gone in that direction. Or better, if his family had a booth somewhere at Taste Fest.

After a brisk run, a lot of shoving and squeezing, I found O. He stood curbside, watching the parade. But he wasn't alone. He stood with a young Asian woman and it looked like they were in a heated discussion. I approached, unable to make her out until I was up close.

He spoke in a gentle, but angry voice.

"Mihoko," O whispered. "I told you it had to stop. Now look what happened. Why are you doing this? Why didn't you listen to me?"

She wore her dark hair twisted into a braid that brushed the side of her neck. I didn't notice it when I was at the restaurant a few nights before, but Mihoko's upper back and arms were covered in scars from an old burn.

A girl in a cheerleading uniform marched by, twirling a baton. Mihoko trained her gaze on the cheerleader and the marching band following closely behind. One of the drummers stopped, drilling his instrument next to Mihoko as if to impress her.

"What are you so worried about? You have your whole life ahead of you," she answered bitterly."

"Not if you keep doing this! You have your whole life ahead of *you too*, Mihoko, why are you throwing it away?"

The girl peered around him and looked right into my face. Strangely, she didn't seem as sweet or as innocent as she did the night I saw her at the restaurant. O followed her gaze. The look in his eyes softened when he realized it was me.

O grabbed my hand and held tight.

"Is everything okay?" I asked.

Her eyes challenged him, daring him to speak.

"I'm just trying to help you," O said.

"There's nothing you can do," Mihoko snapped. "Your mother and father are looking for you. They're on East Patrol, and twelfth. They need someone to watch the booth."

She shrugged, turning to watch the parade again.

His eyes defied her.

"I'm done with the restaurant. Tell them to watch it themselves."

"Of course," Mihoko hissed. "Go ahead and disappoint mommy and daddy again." Her eyes focused directly on me as she spoke.

"You should stay here and work if your parents need you. It's no big deal, you can pick me up when you're done," I offered.

"I'm taking the night off," he said.

"I can wait until you're done," I assured him, determined to make peace. "Go with your sister."

I let him go. I just wanted to make things better.

O shook his head. "*Mihoko*. Tell mother and father I'll see them in a few days."

"A few days?" Mihoko shrieked. Her eyes popped open like he had slapped her across the face. "What does it matter? You'll just do whatever the hell you want anyway."

Mihoko pushed O aside and disappeared into the crowd. He rubbed his forehead like he was getting a headache as a group of revelers pushed and shoved the two of us together until we stood face to face.

"Let's go," O demanded.

"What about Mihoko?"

"Mihoko has done enough," he answered harshly.

"Can we take a walk? You look like your head is about to explode."

"Just don't ask me any questions," O said, hand coming to a rest on his forehead like he was at the end of his rope.

"I won't ask you anything," I assured him in a gentle voice.

He stopped pacing and looked at my face, calming down.

"I'm sorry, I'm just…I'm just tired."

He took my hand again. O and I took a side street to the park and walked to the pier, the tension between us quietly resigned to memory.

"I'm sorry about Mihoko," he said. "And for the way I acted when I was with her."

"It's alright," I answered.

I wanted to know more but had already promised not to ask him about it.

"Mihoko and I used to be close. But things got weird one day so I distanced myself. We hardly talk anymore."

"It's not uncommon to have a bond with your brother or sister. It's actually a good thing, O."

"You don't understand. Mihoko is confused. I don't want to encourage her."

"Confused?"

I tried not to push, O was finally opening up to me.

"She hates every woman I'm with. She hates when I leave town on business. Dealing with her is very difficult. I'm tired."

Blairwood fishing pier extended a block and a half over Lake Michigan, a wooden platform buttressed by pillars that were surrounded on all sides by craggy boulders that descended deep into the water below.

O and I climbed down, jumping from one heavy stone to another until we found a place to sit; on the highest rock, away from the waves crashing below us.

The air was sweet, a mist of lake water cooling

the air…. I curled my legs beneath me and snuggled close, laying my head on O's shoulder as he cradled me in his arms.

"I love my sister but she's dangerous."

"Dangerous how?"

O gave me a squeeze, as if to shield me from the cool lakeside breeze.

"The night we were supposed to go to the prom, Mihoko refused to let me go."

"Why?"

O sighed. "It's complicated."

"Just tell me, O. I promise I won't judge you or Mihoko."

"I know."

He cupped my chin, lifting my face to look him in the eyes then kissed me.

We sat in silence, watching a fisher at the other end of the pier reel in a giant unwanted carp.

"I was supposed to work at the restaurant the night we went to prom but I convinced my parents to let me go. Believe it or not, dating American girls was strictly forbidden. When they finally gave their approval, I could tell Mihoko was unhappy. We were best friends once, always joking around and goofing off with each other, the perfect children of an honorable hard working Japanese-American family until

Mihoko's jealousy broke the bond we shared."

I was afraid to hear the rest. What could break the friendship of two siblings in a close-knit family like O's? I prayed it had nothing to do with me.

"What did Mihoko do?"

"She kissed me."

O looked at me, his eyes filled with regret.

"When it happened I hit her and *said, 'I'm your brother, Mihoko', how can you do this?* She told me she didn't care, that she loved me anyway. I was so infuriated, so repulsed by what she did I almost hit her again but managed to restrain myself. I felt guilty for striking Mihoko and tried to apologize but it was too late…she ran away."

"O, this is crazy. What was she thinking?"

"I wish I knew. It wasn't always like this. She liked a boy once, but my mother said Mihoko wasn't allowed to date."

"Why?"

"She's promised to someone else."

"Like an arranged marriage?"

"Exactly, and she's taking it out on me."

"That's one hell of way to do it!"

"Mihoko's jealous of me. I can be whatever I want, or marry whoever I want while Mihoko is stuck with our family working at the restaurant. I wish things were different for her, but my parents refuse to change their minds. They won't listen to us."

"I still don't understand. Why would she kiss you? What does that have to do with anything?"

"Mihoko's was very young when the *omiai,* was arranged between my parents through the *nakodo.*"

"What's a nakodo?"

"A nakodo is someone who acts as a go-between. He decides the compatibility of the couple and negotiates the terms of an arranged marriage. The future partners must be suitable in every way."

"What do you mean by suitable?"

"They must be healthy, attractive and educated. Arranged marriages are rare, in Japan. The ones that exist are between two adults, with parents on both sides negotiating the terms through the nakodo. But Mihoko's marriage is different. It was decided before she was old enough to object...this arrangement is important to my family. It's tied to one of my father's old gambling debts. Because of the iron clad agreement on both sides, the arrangement cannot be broken unless one of the candidates is no longer suitable. Mental illness would give my sister just the excuse she needed to get the other side to cancel their end of the arrangement and that's why she kissed me. If the engagement is broken, my parents lose everything."

"So Mihoko is playing crazy to get out of an arranged marriage?"

"I don't think she's playing."

"Did you tell your parents what Mihoko was up to? What did they say?"

"On the night of our prom, I told my parents what Mihoko did, but it was already too late. She ran away from the family and got into serious trouble."

I wondered if it had anything to do with the mysterious burns I saw on Mihoko's arms and back.

"I felt guilty for reacting the way I did so I took the blame. I was arrested and sentenced to eight months in jail for Mihoko's crime."

Chapter Seven

O's eyes turned dark, anger blazing within them. Anger, at having said too much already…I dared not ask what Mihoko did, but I knew it was serious. It also explained why O disappeared six years ago, the night of our prom.

"That was a very brave and honorable thing you did for your sister."

We sat facing each other, waves crashing around us.

"You sacrificed your life to save Mihoko. Why would you do that after everything she did to you?"

"She's my sister and I want to protect her."

"From herself?"

The flames in his eyes blazed even hotter.

"From getting hurt again." The grip on my hand tightened. "Are we okay?" O asked.

"Everybody has family problems," I answered, leaning against him as waves crashed ashore.

"Not like mine."

I left my seat on the stone, gazing into brilliant sunlight as an emotionally drained O regrouped. He grabbed my arm and pulled me onto his lap...drawing me close for a kiss. Everything was out in the open now. I felt a sense of closure.

I held O in my arms and he slackened against me, laying his head on my shoulder as if to rest after a long journey. I could feel his strength returning as he pressed his face against the curve of my neck. I tried my best to cleanse my thoughts of Mihoko. But mental images of the young woman kissing her own brother pervaded my thoughts. I could see the pain in his eyes as he told the story of how her actions destroyed their family and how it humiliated him. Suddenly I understood why it had been so difficult to earn his trust.

After the cathartic confession from O, we left the pier and went back to the fest. We watched the rest of the parade and bought goodies, feeling closer than ever, holding hands as we made our way back to O's apartment. It was nice to see him laugh. To see him so relieved. We made it to the building an hour and a half later and took the freight elevator to the fourth floor.

When we arrived at the apartment O opened the

door and gestured for me to go inside.

"I'll be back," he said, standing outside.

"Where are you going?"

He kissed me. "See you in an hour."

He pulled the door and closed it behind him. I waited until he was gone and ran to the bathroom and opened the medicine cabinet. I grabbed the prescription bottle I saw the night before and read the label.

Mihoko had been prescribed anti-depressants by Dr. Shuter.

Dr. Shuter?

The doctor at the hospital clinic…the one I was supposed to see. I had no intention of following through on the appointment at first, but it seemed I had more than enough reason to visit him now.

I got comfortable, and changed out of hot street clothes into one of O's shirts, a white button down. Then I searched the apartment. I looked for anything that would give me clues about his past and the time he spent in jail. I wanted information about his family's restaurant, old debts. I needed <u>evidence</u>. Could that be the reason why O refused to tell me his real name? He knew I would have access to his records using the Madison Heights Police database. That I would learn the truth.

I went back to the culinary certificate on O's wall and pulled the push pins out. I tried to read his name, but it was written in Kanji, a Chinese influenced Japanese alphabet system. I was expecting the rest of the certificate to be written in English, but I was wrong…about everything.

After exploring the cabinets and drawers, I looked under the bed. I searched envelopes and documents, most of which were also written in Japanese. Then I carefully put everything back in place, including a skewed picture frame on the wall. I tilted it sideways again, after knocking it straight by mistake.

I checked under the sofa, in old bags and backpacks, and finally the closet shelves. Buried under a pile of neatly folded jeans was an old shoebox.

I sat on the floor, the box between my legs. What was inside? Lifting the lid, I found a stack of dirty magazines. A busty Nubian-esque model posed in scanty swimwear that barely covered her voluptuous buttocks. Bastard! Why is he looking at all of these women? I took Nubian Babe out of the shoebox and set it on top of a stack of similar magazines.

Delving further, I found a wad of money, a set of strange looking keys, a stack of 20 euro in bills, and three diamonds that must have been worth a fortune.

Then I saw it…the photograph. And suddenly my hands were shaking as I took it out of the shoebox. It was a picture of me in a cheerleading uniform, standing next to O at our old high school. My arms were around his neck, my lips pressed warmly against his cheek. A hot stream of tears poured out of my eyes. I traced a finger along our faces, trying to imagine how many times he'd taken it out of the box and held it in his hands. Guilt pricked the back of my conscience. What was I doing? I kissed the picture, my lips against O's face, then gathered the contents of the box and put them in order again. I was about to put everything back where I got it from when I noticed something at the very bottom of the box. I took the item out and held it in my quivering hand.

It was a video tape with 5/12 written on the side of it. I tried to breathe through the sob locked in my throat. 5/12 was the date of the fire at the Pancake House. It was a surveillance tape.

A deluge of tears poured out of my eyes as I finally realized the truth.

If O had nothing to do with the fires, then what was he doing with the tape? Why was he lurking around the Pancake House after it burned down? And why was his family's restaurant the only one to survive the arsons? Was he really in love with me? Or staying close to keep an eye on the investigation?

I left the shoe box on the floor, scurried across the room and grabbed my purse, stuffing the evidence inside. I pushed it to the bottom under a clattering of makeup, my wallet, and checkbook. I had to get the tape to Dana. I snatched my jeans and slid into them, hoping for a fast getaway when I heard O's key sliding into the door.

I rushed across the room, my heart slamming back and forth against my ribcage as I scrambled to put everything back where I got it. I kicked the shoebox into the closet, leaving the pile of jeans that concealed the sloppy mess. The sleeve of one of his shirts hung through a crack in the door. A clear indication that his things had been rummaged through. I prayed he wouldn't notice.

O walked in, his smiling face quickly turning to stone. He walked across the room, each methodical step drawing us closer and closer to disaster. I pulled myself together, lifting my eyes to his face. He stood before me, the corner of his dangerously kissable lips turning upward into a faux smile.

My pulses raced and tears blurred my eyes. I

wanted to speak, but could only gulp air as I struggled to confront the man I loved about the arsons. Then I remembered what Dana told me… *'Don't blow the investigation'.*

"What's wrong?" O asked, lips drawing into a tight white line. His eyes scanned the room then landed on my face again. The energy between us had suddenly changed. The familiarity between us completely lost.

"I'm sorry, I…have to go," I gasped.

"Go where?"

He looked disappointed.

"There's an emergency at home," I replied in an eerily calm voice… certain, however, I looked anything but calm.

"Is that what you're so upset about? *Were you crying?*"

He cupped my chin. The softness of my cheeks sunk under his fingertips. I drew my purse from the bed, holding tight.

O shook his head.

"First, you need to calm down," he replied. "Sit and have some tea with me before you go."

"I can't…"

"We need to talk."

"About what?" I asked.

His voice was silky smooth, "You're running away."

O wiped a tear from my face. I melted on the inside, wondering if his warm, loving hands were capable of helping Mihoko start a fire that killed a man.

"I'm not running," I answered calmly.

"Well, you can't go out there like that."

O gestured towards a chair at the dining room table. I sat down, though wanting to bolt out the door.

He went to the stove with a kettle of water. I watched as he mixed ingredients together then settled the tea leaves into a fancy handcrafted Japanese teapot. After the water had reached its boiling point, he poured the steamy liquid over the mixture.

My tensing muscles relaxed as an intoxicating aroma filled my nostrils. We were silent as he poured the brew into teacups.

O slid the warm invigorating drink to my side of the table, eyes flicking over my face. I gave a pretense of trust and calm as my eyes met his.

We sipped from the ceramic teacups at the same time, eyes locked across the table. "This is the tea we drank the first night at your apartment."

I looked into my cup where a tiny white flower had bloomed on the inside from the mixture.

"It's called raspberry cherry blossom. It's a blooming tea."

I inhaled, drawing a gulp of air as a cool menthol sensation flowed from my lungs into my nostrils, setting my cheeks aglow...a sensation that flowed into every limb in my body. I felt loose and nimbly. O blinked, staring calmly at my face.

"Are you okay?" he asked.

I sank into my chair, breaths heavy. "I can't breathe," I muttered, holding my chest.

"It's just the tea," he said. "Don't worry."

O stood, pulled my chair back, and kneeled beside me, a cold look in his eyes.

"I work with an overseas laboratory testing chemicals in different food products. I have accounts in Japan and Europe. We don't have to be apart, I promise", he said, stroking my cheeks.

And then there were two of him as my vision blurred.

"How much do you weigh, Victoria? I think the concoction was a little strong for you...I just wanted to help you calm down. It'll pass...I promise."

My limbs slackened. I sunk further, and slipped from the seat into his arms. "I love you, O. I prayed it wasn't you."

Tears sprang into the corners of my eyes and rolled down my cheeks. I felt the wind under my feet as he drew me into his arms and carried me off to bed.

Physically, I was numb, unable to move I stole at a look into O's eyes.

"You're supposed to drink it slow," he said, brushing hair away from my face. He shook his head. "You drink too fast."

"What did you give me?" I asked in a shrinking voice.

His eyes softened. "An herb. I made it special, just for you."

Chapter Eight

I awakened hours later to the sterile medicinal smell of a hospital room and my parents hovering above me with worried looks on their faces. I moaned. My muscles ached and my eyes were under assault from the bright halogen lamp aimed at my forehead. This wasn't a dream…I was actually in the hospital. I bolted upright, as memories of what happened at O's apartment came crashing back, a sharp pain striking the front of my head at the same time.

"Lay down!" mother cried, drawing the hospital blanket up to my neck. "Ain't no telling what he did to you."

Dana and Daniel the fire chief was there. They sat bedside for hours, waiting for me to wake up. What had Daniel to do with any of this? He was the fire chief. His part of the investigation was over.

"What am I doing here? Where's O?" I asked.

"In jail, where he ought to be."

I read the anger in my mother's voice loud and clear, but she was wrong, O would never do anything to hurt me.

"What happened?"

"We saw everything," Dana said. "We've had him under surveillance for the past few days. Forensics came back with positive results on a cigarette butt we found at the crime scene and one the suspect tossed on the pavement when he picked you up the other day. We also ID'd him in the videotape you found in his apartment."

"You guys were watching us the entire time?"

Dana's face turned three degrees of red. "Not the entire time," she answered. "You did good, Tai. You brought a killer to justice."

And yet, I didn't feel good. I felt like any woman would feel after betraying the man she loved. I shook my head, still bewildered by the turn of events.

"I can't believe it. I don't want to..." I muttered absently.

"I'm sorry," Dana said. "I wish it was different, I really do."

I felt the weight of the world on my shoulders as I sat in bed trying to take it all in. The last thing I remembered was drinking the tea O had given me and falling asleep.

"Why am I here?"

"Dr. Michaels took blood and ran a few tests. Whatever the suspect put in that drink knocked you out cold."

"O would *never*…do anything to hurt me. And stop calling him a suspect! He didn't do it…"

I couldn't' believe they were making him out to be some type of predator. I was certain – if it wasn't a mistake, there was a very good reason for what he did.

My father paced the room. He hated the idea of knowing I spent the past few days at O's apartment. Alone.

"Hija, what were you doing with this…*criminal!*" father spat. "You know nothing about this man. It's over now. So let's just put it behind us move on," he grumbled uncomfortably.

"And what if I don't want to move on?" I shot back.

A collective quiet washed across the room. I was sick of everyone tiptoeing around the conversation. *What weren't they telling me?*

Dana sighed. She sat on the edge of my hospital bed, covering my hand with her own.

"His name is Yoshihiro Otari."

The shock of hearing his name for the first time reverberated to the core of my being. I felt robbed. I wanted to find out on my own or wait for O to reveal it himself.

"He told you his real name?"

"We knew it all along. He was arrested six years ago for starting the fire that injured his sister. As a first time offender, the judge reduced his sentence. His family also refused to press charges. He was released eight months later and moved to Japan where he went to college and majored in Biochemistry. After he graduated, he moved back home and took a job at Gresham University teaching an agricultural biochemistry course. He's a top of the line chef because of his scientific background and his ability to bring different elements together. He mixed herbs in the tea, which allowed him to render you unconscious. We were watching from the building across the street. When I saw you collapse, I knew he'd given you something. So we raided the apartment and placed him under arrest."

"Can I see him?"

"After everything he did to you?" mother shrieked. "Absolutely, not."

"I swear mom, he wasn't trying to hurt me."

Dana gripped my hand, her voice gentle, "A man died, Tai. Yoshihiro will be in jail for a very long time. Probably for the rest of his natural life…"

The fires started a few months ago, not long

after O returned. The evidence was stacked against him and yet, it still didn't make sense. Why did he set the fires? What was the motive?

"I'm not ready to believe that yet."

I found the man I loved and lost him again and it was entirely my own fault. I planted myself into O's life under the guise of being with him again. I wasn't sure at the time whether I wanted it to work between us or not. But now that he was locked away in jail, where I would never see him again, the answer was as clear as a blue sky. At the apartment, I was afraid to hear the truth…but not anymore. The O I knew wasn't a thrill seeker who got off on setting fires. It wasn't in his nature. He was calm, patient, and quiet…and when we were alone, the most passionate man I had ever met. He loved to create, not destroy. Why would a serial arsonist who burned restaurants to the ground, choose to become a chef?

O told me he went to jail for his sister's crime six years ago. He also told me that she hated working at the family restaurant. He told me she was dangerous, angry, and wanted to be free.

What if Mihoko set the fires?

Chapter Nine

After another twenty-four hours in the hospital for observation, the doctor finally signed my release. The herbs O put in the tea were harmless and legal, despite the sedative-like side effects. A battery of tests revealed that I was in good health, though the doctor advised a follow-up appointment at his clinic in a few weeks. My HCG levels were a bit high but he told me it was probably nothing to worry about. It may have something to do with the herbs in O's tea.

Mother and father wheeled me out of the hospital to a waiting van despite my eagerness to walk on my own. But I knew, the moment I set foot on the pavement, I couldn't make it without their help. My legs were still wobbly and weak.

All I could think about was getting well, so I could plead O's innocence to Dana before the case was sent to the D.A. But how could I effectively defend O without Dana firing back that I was doing it because I loved him?

As I lay in bed at the hospital with nothing but time on my hands and a thirteen inch TV with a bad speaker, I pieced the facts together. O was intensely protective of his family and was willing to take the rap for Mihoko's crime, just as he had done six years ago.

Weeks before the prom, O had gotten permission from his parents to not only attend, but to take me as his date. That night, a jealous Mihoko rebelled against the double standards her family had shown the siblings and kissed her own brother. O sent her away in anger, and Mihoko started her first fire. She was injured in the process, which resulted in the burns I saw on her arm and neck. O not only felt guilty but was urged by his parents to accept responsibility for her crimes...somehow, to protect the family and Mihoko's arranged marriage. He slipped away before the police caught him and met me by the pond at the back of my parent's house to say goodbye. We spent the next few hours in each other's arms, until the police showed up and O fled. He was arrested and sent to jail where he served eight months. I met Everett while he was away. When O got out of jail he came back for me but learned Everett and I were together. So he moved to Japan in vain, where he went to college, having achieved his high school diploma in absentia the last two weeks of school. O lived in Japan for five years. Took a job in Europe, and then moved back to the states. When he returned, Mihoko reacted, and the fires started again. Or was I grasping at straws? All I needed was a motive. Why would Mihoko set the fires after her brother returned but not during the six years he was away? There was more to their relationship than O had been willing to share. I remembered the conversation I overheard when he spoke to Mihoko on the phone…and then there was the jade comb at the Pancake House the day after the fire. O went back to the restaurant to get rid of it, once again, trying to help his sister. But how could I explain his presence at the restaurant the night before?

I had to see the tape.

Chapter Ten

When I got to Shima's on Saturday, Jonathan Lewis was waiting for me at the bar. He nursed a tumbler of scotch, cigar couched between two of his fingers, a thick band of smoke wafting over his head. When he saw me walking towards him, he smiled like a cat with a bird in its mouth. I wore a scorching red mini dress and heels, my thick mane of hair already growing back in, swept to the side, drew appreciative looks from just about anyone with two legs and a mustache. Jonathan waved the bartender over as I sat on the stool beside him.

"A dry martini, hold the olive, please."

The bartender complied, returning in mere seconds with my drink. He sat it on a napkin, sweeping the bar with a towel, as he turned away.

"I heard you were in the hospital. We can do this some other time," Jonathan started.

"Don't worry about it, I'm fine!" I replied,

shrugging him off with an air of cool.

I checked my lipstick, using a compact mirror from my clutch. Jonathan smiled like he was ready to devour me whole as I plied my lips with color.

The editor stood about as tall as O, with a short dark afro cut to precision and facial hair that had been fashioned into a goatee. He had broad shoulders, muscular thighs and a wide chest…wide enough to lay my head against and sob my heart out. I had no one to talk to. Dana was keeping a distance and the man I loved was in jail.

I'd made a mess of my investigation and a mess of the article I was supposed to write. The last thing I wanted to do was make O look guilty.

"The reason I invited you out to dinner…"

I cut Jonathan off, waving a hand… "I can't write the article."

"What?"

"They arrested the wrong guy."

Jonathan chomped the end of his cigar, a look of surprise on his face.

"But he drugged you."

"I can't explain why he'd do something like that. I don't have all the answers. His sister Mihoko started the fires. Yoshihiro is trying to protect her, lord knows why."

I sipped the martini, my empty stomach releasing a growl.

"And you're convinced of this...*why*?"

"He alluded to serving eight months in jail for a crime his sister committed six years ago. Mihoko was apparently in love with her own brother. The girl is just plain confused."

"So you have a string of arsons, an incestuous romance , and possible insurance fraud... which could be at the crux of the whole ordeal."

"What insurance fraud?"

"The Otari family is being sued by the IRS. They need money. *Bad*."

"And you think they were going to torch their own restaurant and blame it on the arsons?"

Jonathan nodded. "I'll give you time if you need it, but don't get hurt again. Understood?"

A waiter met us at the bar... our table was finally ready. My stomach growled in anticipation. The waiter took us across the room and we sat down. I paged through the menu and told the young man what I wanted. Jonathan ordered a bottle of chardonnay. We sipped wine as we waited for dinner to arrive.

I tried to figure out a way to tell Jonathan about the difficulties I was having with the department. I'd reached an impasse. Dana was so worried about me compromising the investigation, that she used my time in the hospital to suggest a leave of absence citing a technicality in department policy. I was injured in the line of duty and that itself required a separate investigation even though I was a civilian employee and not an officer. Our friendship had become somewhat estranged in the past 48 hours and O was at the center of our rift. She was forcing me to choose between my best friend and the man I loved.

"There's a tape. I found it the night Yoshihiro was arrested. But it was taken by the department. I've been effectively blocked from having access to any of the evidence."

The waiter arrived with dinner, setting our plates before us. I turned mine clockwise, trying to decide where to dig in.

"There's a conflict of interest, my job at the paper and all," I fibbed. "Is there something we could use, like freedom of the press, to gain access to the tape? I think the video will prove my suspicions about Mihoko right."

Jonathan cut into the salmon hibachi on his plate.

"I can get the tape."

"How soon?"

"I'll call you as soon as it's in my possession."

I sighed in relief. "The case is going to the DA as soon as the rest of the evidence is in. An innocent man could spend the rest of his life in prison. "

"We'll get the tape, don't worry. "

Jonathan looked at me, his eyebrows furrowing together anxiously.

"About tonight…the reason I invited you to dinner…"

"I thought you invited me here to talk about the arson case?" I gave him a thoughtful look.

Jonathan smiled. "I'd like to offer you a full-time job at the paper."

"What?"

"Our lead political analyst is retiring. I want you to take her place."

I pushed my chicken tempura aside and stared at Jonathan, completely stunned. "I'm beyond flattered…" I gasped.

Only, I wasn't exactly a follower of local politics. So why was he offering the position to me?

"If you accept, you can't moonlight at the station anymore. It's a full-time gig."

"I appreciate the offer," I said, chewing my bottom lip nervously… "I really do but…"

"No buts!" Jonathan answered, waving a hand as he stuffed a bite of salmon into his mouth.

"You start in a week. There's a party next Friday at Senator Grayson's house. I want you to go with me. I'll introduce you to some of our insiders and a few well connected friends. It's easier to write about people when you know them."

"It sounds awesome," I muttered. "Bu..." I opened my mouth to speak but Jonathan interrupted.

"Then you accept? Good. I was hoping you'd say yes."

I swallowed nervously. It was my dream come true, a full-time job at the paper! As much as I liked working at the department with Dana, my faith in the girl had been shaken to the core. Dana treated me like I couldn't be trusted anymore. She refused to talk about O's case. Jonathan was my only hope. He could get the tape.

"Get the arson story finished as soon as you can and I'll have my assistant get in touch with you next week. You'll need to meet with HR to discuss salary expectations and other personnel matters."

Jonathan reached across the table, extending a hand. I grabbed it, accepting the congratulatory handshake. "Good to have you aboard, Tai."

He gazed at my face, eyes twinkling as he lowered his head and kissed the back of my hand before letting it go.

The imprint of his lips made my skin tingle.

We ate the rest of our meal, enjoying the chic but subtle ambiance of Shima's. An eastern inspired design decorated the partition that separated the private area we sat in from the open plan kitchen and sushi counter. There was spacious seating, a pond with trickling water that sounded like a babbling brook, with live fish swimming around inside of it.

I looked up to catch Jonathan checking my ring hand.

"I'm not married," I volunteered.

"I'm surprised some lucky guy hasn't snapped you up."

"Like trout? No lucky guys yet. I'm in a relationship but things are complicated... actually, we're teetering on an ugly break up. "

"That bad, huh? I know how it is. I'm recently divorced."

"I'm sorry."

"It happens," he shrugged. "How's the food?"

I thought about the rich gourmet food O cooked for us at his apartment.

"Good. But I've had better."

"That's too bad. I was hoping we could do this again."

"I'm not opposed to it," I smiled. "It's a lovely place."

Jonathan's hand swept over mine, tracing the curves along the lines of my hand.

"Tell me about your boyfriend."

I sighed, breathing dreamily as I rested my chin on top of my other hand. "We met in high school. He was my first love."

"Your first love!" Jonathan hung his head. "I don't stand a chance, do I?"

I giggled, rolling my eyes. "Let's talk about something else, alright?"

"Agreed!"

We finished our respective meals. When I was done with the chicken tempura, I followed it with a serving of hamachi and lemon torte cakes, one right after the other.

I licked my fingers then looked up at Jonathan's grinning face.

"What are you smiling at?" I asked, sweeping the last square of cake into my mouth.

"You're really packing that stuff away."

I also demolished a tray of expensive sashimi appetizers when we first sat down. When how much I'd actually eaten dawned on me, I wanted to die I was so embarrassed. Jonathan smiled as I resisted the urge to burp away the cake that dropped into the empty cavern of my bottomless stomach!

He finished his Salmon Hibachi and poured

the last of the chardonnay into our glasses. Jonathan teased me relentlessly about the food I'd eaten, calling me "Sushi" the rest of the night. I laughed so hard I was sick.

But my laughter swiftly succumbed to silence, when the investigation came up again. Jonathan went on and on about it, highlighting his suspicions and things he'd heard through a source at the station. I pushed my plate away and looked down, finger tracing the edge of my wineglass. Sensing the change in mood, Jonathan stretched across the table, hand cupping my chin.

I met his lovely dark brown eyes.

"Let's get out of here," he whispered, in a somber voice.

Jonathan paid the bill and escorted me out of the restaurant to the valet, who quickly retrieved his car. "Thank you, Mr. Lewis," the young man said with a familiar grin, handing Jonathan the keys to a sleek, brand new Genesis Coupe.

He followed me to the passenger side of the car and opened the door. I sat down, slightly buzzed from the wine. Jonathan climbed into the driver's seat moments later.

"Let's go to the park," I suggested.

"What's at the park?"

"Peace and quiet," I sighed.

He turned off. We went to the capital and toured the outside of the building until we found a place to sit. We rested on the stone surround of a massive fountain with the statue of an angel cradling two cherubs on a raised plateau, water cascading down into the pond below where a dazzling array of lights blinked on and off. Jonathan and I sat side by side, plastic coffee cups in hand.

"I'm glad we did this. It's nice."

Somehow, between talking about O and the investigation, Jonathan managed to take my mind off of my problems.

"Me too," Jonathan replied.

He took my hand and we walked to the car, enjoying the warm evening breeze.

Jonathan drove me home. When we arrived, he parked in my parent's driveway, the glow of a street lamp pouring in for light as we talked about the future and my new job at Journal.

"You're a reporter. Your job is to observe and give an accurate account of newsworthy events. If Yoshihiro's sister is guilty of starting the fires, the police will get to the bottom of it."

I couldn't tell him what I knew about O…that he was more than willing to take the blame for his sister's crime and that a murderer was running loose in our city. Who knew when she'd burn something else and kill again? Could be days or even years from now…and then it would be too late.

"Why did you pick me for the political analyst job? I have no experience to speak of and I'm only a couple of years out of college."

Jonathan frowned. "You're talking me out of it, now…"

"Seriously…"

"You're gorgeous and I like you…And that's all you need to know," he grinned.

I gripped his hand. "I want you to like me for my writing."

"I like that too."

My stomach churned and my head began to throb. I clutched my side, bending forward.

"I'm going inside. Remind me to *never* drink like that again."

Jonathan smiled and pulled me close. I pressed my palm against his chest. We were so close I could smell the touch of musk in his cologne.

Jonathan's hand slid to my left thigh and the other dropped to the small of my back. He leaned across the console. I gazed into his eyes, drawn to the sensual parting of his mouth as his lips moved towards mine.

"What are you doing?"

Jonathan made a grim face. "I misread something, didn't I?"

I laughed. "I'm sorry. I wasn't trying to send mixed signals."

"Don't worry, I forgive you," he smiled.

"You forgive *me*?" I gasped. "You're supposed to be my new boss, remember?"

"Ah ...*that*," he replied, the sound of regret in his voice.

I reached for the lock and the car door plunked open. I slithered out and scurried onto the driveway of my parent's house, took my shoes off, and carried them to the door.

I stuck my key into the lock and backed into the house. Once inside, I went to the window and pulled a sliver of curtain back to see if Jonathan was gone. I watched as he sped away.

My stomach revolted, churning and rumbling painfully as I made my way upstairs. I collapsed on the cold bathroom floor and stuck my head in the toilet, puking my face off. When I was done, I sat on the floor, waiting for the next wave nausea to hit.

The next day, the doorbell rang bright and early. Mom was in the kitchen scrambling eggs. I wanted to regurgitate as I stumbled out of bed and went downstairs.

A courier had arrived with a package from

Jonathan. I tore it open the second I closed the door and ran upstairs to my mother's room to use her VHS player. There was a tape inside of the box.

I put it in, my stomach a bundle of nerves as images of customers going in and out of the Pancake House on the day of the fire appeared on the screen.

I sat on the edge of mom's bed. Seconds later, she walked in and sat down.

"What is it?" mom asked, leaning over my shoulder.

"It's a tape. "

"You think! What's on it?"

"A murder."

Mother frowned, dimples creasing her kewpie-like face.

"Like an actual snuff tape? Oh, Victoria! I don't want it in my room! Get out of here with that!"

I pointed the remote control in my hand.

"It's not a snuff tape. Remember the arson case? Police saw O at the restaurant on the surveillance tape. But he left thirty minutes before the fire started."

"So he killed somebody, just like Dana said!"

"O wouldn't hurt a fly."

I pointed the remote, fast forwarding.

Mother's soaps were about to come on, I had to get through as much of the six hour video as I could. The only VHS in the house was built into her television.

Mother fluffed her pillows and curled up, watching the video with me.

"Slow down, I can't see anything."

"What about your soaps?"

"Never mind the soaps, let's see what's on that tape."

I was afraid of what I was about to see, but love was an act of faith, I knew in my heart O was incapable of burning a restaurant down, much less killing a man. Dana was suspicious because of the time he spent in jail six years ago for an arson he didn't even commit and I was determined to prove her wrong.

"I could do this all day," mom said, breaking into my thoughts.

Mom was a fan of mystery novels and thought herself an amateur detective. She watched CSI shows and forensic crime documentaries. Of course, in her mind that meant she was a "qualified forensic scientist."

"Who died?"

"The manager..."

"Poor guy. He was just doing his job!" she cried.

I grabbed the remote control and fast forwarded as close as I could get to the end of the tape without feeling like I was about to miss something important. As I suspected, a woman who looked like Mihoko entered the restaurant thirty minutes before close time. I could only see her from behind, but I knew it was her.

According to the time stamp, O walked in twenty minutes later. He wore a dark leather jacket, the same one he'd worn the next day when I met him at the Pancake House. The grainy black and white footage showed him going to the manager's office. Three customers sat scattered across the restaurant. One man drank coffee and read the paper. A woman who looked to be in her thirties ate a slice of pie and twirled coins. A man in a thick leather jacket and a pair of dark shades sat near the window. I looked for Mihoko.

It seemed strange, that O would draw attention to himself in that way if he was planning to start a fire knowing the poor restaurant manager was still inside. I suspected, the man in the leather jacket was a plant from police department keeping an eye on things. His body language screamed "undercover cop." But where was he when the fire started?

Ten minutes after O went into the man's

office, the manager came out. A light fixture in the ceiling flickered and dimmed as the manager curled around to the front counter and talked to the waitress, a slender woman of sixty with a large bouffant hairdo. When they were done, he kissed her on the lips. She stroked his arms and he spun away, retreating to his office again.

The waitress peeked through a partition and looked into the kitchen where the cook was cleaning up for the night. She waved him over. The man took his apron off, tossed it under the counter and went home for the night.

A few minutes later, O came out and the manager escorted him to the door. The man in the leather jacket got up, following O. Now, there were only two customers left.

The waitress scampered over to the table where the old man was sitting and collected his empty coffee cup and saucer. The man laid his newspaper down and got up a few minutes later. He left the restaurant, waving "goodbye" as he went out the door. And then there was one.

The woman with the coin was ushered out with a foam container for her pie.

When the customers were finally gone, the waitress went to the back and knocked on the manager's door. He came out and there was an argument. The flustered looking waitress began to cry. But the manager stood firm, marching her to the door…holding it open for her as she walked out.

Not long after everyone, including waitress, was out of the building did flames explode out of a side window and plumes of smoke rose to the sky. I leaned close to the television and watched the blazing fire. "What happened to Mihoko?" I asked, thinking aloud.

"You mean the girl in the white sweater?"

I jerked as though I had been startled awake. I forgot mom was in the room.

"I saw her go in…but didn't see her come out," I mused.

"She went out the side window," mom replied in a superior tone, like I was crazy for missing it.

"What?"

"Right before the explosion. Blink and you miss it!"

She pointed a finger at the TV.

"The glass on the side of the building shattered because of the heat."

"I saw her clear as day a few seconds before the explosion. Rewind the tape!" She was on her feet, excited now.

I did as mother asked. On the other side of the restaurant, almost out of the camera's line of view, did someone appear. It was hard to make out because of the smoke. Flames from the ever spreading fire blocked the only exit.

The lights in the diner flickered and went dark, making it easy to miss the young woman in the white sweater as she grabbed a chair and bashed it against the window. What happened next had been obscured by the explosion.

"This is insane! O wasn't there! So why is he in jail? The guy in the leather jacket was a detective. He followed O out of the restaurant. They know he didn't start the fire. And here's the kicker… O and I were together that night! The time code on the tape showed O leaving the restaurant at 10:45. O was at our house a little after 11pm. We were well on our way to his apartment when the fire started. There has to be video of us somewhere!"

"Did you stop for gas?"

"No. But if I'm lucky there's a video camera in O's building."

I slammed the remote on mom's bed, grabbed the tape and stormed out.

"Where are you going?" mom called.

"To the station! I *have* to see O."

"And what was he doing in our house?"

"I'll tell you about it later," I called.

I tried to visit O on Sundays and Tuesdays, his

visitation days three weeks in a row. But he refused to see me. Was he angry that I searched his apartment and confiscated the tape without his permission? As much as I loathe admitting it, I could hardly blame him if he was. I raced to my bedroom and called the only person who could help. I'd get into the jail one way or another to see him.

"Jonathan," the velvety voice on the other end of the line answered.

"I need your help," I said.

"Did you get the tape?"

"Yes! But I have to talk to the suspect. Can you get me in?"

"I can probably get something arranged with my contact. How soon?"

"In an hour."

"I'll see what I can do."

I changed out of my pajamas and showered as quickly as I could. A cab arrived twenty minutes later. I rode downtown to the station, got out of the car, and waited outside for Jonathan's call. It didn't matter to me that I still looked a mess after days of nausea and insomnia that left bags under my eyes. The tape proved O's innocence and I wanted him out of jail and back in my arms…especially since I was the one who put him there.

I answered my cell on the first ring after pacing outside of the station for ten minutes. Traffic was loud, I could barely hear the voice on the other end of the line so I plugged a finger in one ear and pressed the headpiece against the other.

"He's not there," Jonathan said.

"What!"

"The DA rejected the case. The case against Yoshihiro was paper thin, all of it circumstantial… MHPD released him from jail four days ago."

My body shook so violently that I sat on the steps at the bottom of rotunda to get my bearings. I was elated! Overjoyed that an innocent man, the man I loved was free... until it dawned on me, that he was released four days ago.

Suddenly, grief struck me so hard, and with so much force I felt like the wind had been vacuumed out of my lungs.

"Hello?" Jonathan said.

I'd forgotten he was still on the line.

Crying was the last thing I wanted to do, but tears washed into my eyes. I stood, gripping the hand railing as I walked upstairs to the station where Dana's office was located. Did he really hate me so much that he would get out of jail four days ago without a word?

"Are you alright?" Jonathan asked.

The sound of his voice rang hollow in my ear. I

swiped a tear from my eye, muffling a sob. "I'm fine," I answered, in a voice brimming with faux cheer. "Just a little surprised."

"Sorry about your story, hun."

"I'm not done with my investigation," I spat, surprised he'd thought such a thing. I calmed down, moderating the tone of my voice.

"What do you mean?"

"I'm convinced Mihoko is behind the arsons..."

"If you can finish your piece, that's great! Otherwise, it's time to move on. I'll give you two days."

"Can do. *Jonathan?*"

"What's up?"

"I need a favor."

"Yeah, and what else is new?" he answered dryly. I could hear the smile behind his voice.

"Can you give me a ride to the clinic tomorrow? Dr. Michaels asked me to come in."

"Is it serious?"

"My HCG levels were a little high."

"Not pre-cancerous, *high*?"

"No, of course not. It's just a follow up appointment."

"I'll be there. What time?"

"1:15."

"See you then."

I put my cell phone away and continued up the

stairs to Dana's office. I entered the station. Halls I walked hundreds of times looked alien to me now, after only a month away from the building. I hoped Dana was willing to put our differences behind us now that the investigation was complete. She hated O…that much I knew. But enough to end our friendship? If so, then maybe we were never friends to begin with.

Dana sat in the corner, behind the walls of her cubicle, face submerged in a manila file folder.

I slipped through the partition and eased into the seat behind her.

"Working on anything new?"

Dana kept her head immersed in the paperwork on her desk.

"Who wants to know?" she grunted over her shoulder.

"A friend," I smiled.

"Oh really?"

Tension permeated the room. I could hear the surliness in her voice.

"The investigation's over. Your boy walked."

Dana slammed the manila folder in a drawer and slammed it closed.

"I know," I answered, then after a pause, added . "But he deserved to be free…he didn't do it, Dana…"

Tears pricked the corner of my eyes. Dana

grumbled under her breath, pressing a hand against her temple like it pained her to see me miserable.

"You love him so much, but Yoshihiro's not *here*. He left the country right after his release. There was nothing we could do to stop him."

I faced the brunt of this news with as much dignity as I could muster. Would another six years pass by before I see him again?

"His sister started the fires."

"But did she act alone?"

"We were together the night the Pancake House burned down."

"I know. An investigator followed him to your house."

"If you knew, why did you have O arrested?"

"Obstruction of justice. We did our best to put the fear of God in him, but he refused to sing."

"Mihoko's dangerous. She'll kill again if she's not arrested."

"I talked to the victim's wife…she's a waitress at the Pancake House."

I recalled the waitress who cleared everyone out of the restaurant that night and her reaction when she was asked to leave.

"The night of the murder, Yoshihiro went to her husband's office. He told him to stay alert…he believed the Pancake House was next. They closed early and Mr. Cole stayed behind. Poor guy made the mistake of falling asleep in his office, and it cost him his life."

"Why didn't she go to the police with this information?"

"One could ask the same of Yoshihiro."

"Remember the Jade comb? Did you test it for Mihoko's DNA?"

"We're working on it now. We had Yoshihiro's DNA from his previous arrest. We have nothing on record for his sister, but it's only a matter of days before we close our end of the investigation. The DA's not taking any chances. We need the white sweater she wore the night of the fire."

"I can get it for you."

"Stay out of it, Tai." She pressed her eyebrows together, worriedly. *"Are you sick?"*

I drew a deep breath, unwilling to tell Dana what I had been unwilling to admit to myself.

"Oh dear lord," Dana gasped, a look of realization dawning on her face. She wiped a hand across her forehead nervously. *"How many weeks?"*

"I don't know," I answered, shoulders shrinking. "Dana…I'm such an idiot…I'll never see him again," I cried.

Dana crouched next to my chair, a consoling arm across my shoulders. "There…there," she cooed, patting my back in an awkward display of affection. "We'll figure something out."

She gave me a tissue and I blew my nose, honking it loudly.

"For fucks' sake, Tai. What will your mother say? She's going to have a fit!"

"I don't care. I'm getting my own apartment...and --I wouldn't be the first woman to have a kid by herself."

"On a part-time salary?" Her green penetrating eyes were full of doom.

"Jonathan offered me a full-time job at the paper. It's not a ton of money, but it's enough to get by. When I'm further along, I'll work from home."

"So you're keeping it?"

"I don't' know if I'm pregnant yet. I have morning sickness, I can't keep anything down and I haven't had my period... I have an appointment with Dr. Michaels tomorrow. I won't make a decision until then."

"It sounds like your mind is already made up to me!"

"We'll see."

****

Jonathan arrived at 1:15, as scheduled, dressed like a college professor in a corduroy sports coat, a pair of khakis, and leather red wing shoes. I watched from the window as he walked up the driveway and rang the bell.

"It's him," Mom called, excited to meet the man whom I'd simply described as my boss. When I told my parents about my new job, they did a happy dance around the living room. I watched, knowing their joy would be short-lived.

The door sprang opened. Mom moved aside, looking Jonathan up and down with an air of approval on her face as he walked in.

"Is Victoria home?" Jonathan asked, his larger-than-life presence filling the doorway. I imagined him with his leather briefcase, coming home from work, sweeping me into his arms…then quickly blinked the inappropriate image out of my head.

"Yes she is. I'm Marjorie Lawford, can I get you something to drink?" Mom asked, smiling ear to ear.

He waved her off. There was nothing stiff enough or old enough in the house for a man like Jonathan to imbibe.

She gestured towards the sofa and they sat down, mom with an appreciative sigh.

"So!" she exclaimed, clasping her hands tidily across her lap. "We finally meet!"

"Right…you must be Victoria's *sister*?"

"Oh stop! You don't really mean…*do I really*? Oh!"

Mom snapped her head back and laughed like it was the funniest thing she had ever heard. "Oh gosh, you're cute." My father was the only man she ever truly loved and still, she was a shameless flirt.

I'm Jonathan Lewis, nice to meet you," he said, his voice a rich baritone.

"The pleasure is all mine," mother cooed. She looked towards the stairs with a smile to show me how impressed she was. It wouldn't be the first time she tried to play match maker, even with the understanding that this man was my new boss.

"How long have you worked for the paper?" mom asked.

"Eleven years."

"Forgive my ignorance, but what exactly does a newspaper editor do? Is it writing articles, or editing content?"

"At a newspaper, a copy editor is responsible for grammar and spelling. I'm editor-in-chief of the *Journal* which means I'm responsible for our budget, overseeing content, staffing, managing our writers and mid-level editors. It's different at every paper. At mine, I'm the guy everyone calls *the boss*."

"Nothin' wrong with that," Marjorie offhandedly replied. "What'd you do before that?"

Jonathan smiled. The man's patience was remarkable…mom was one step away from taking his social security number.

"I ran an investment firm. Lewis and Coates."

"Oh, I'll have to look that up. They made a ton of money, didn't they?" she asked, raising a brow.

Jonathan not only ran an investment firm, but had become quite wealthy as a result. He even wrote investment articles for the Business section of the Journal before he was made Editor-in-Chief five years ago.

"Nice…" Marjorie muttered absently, dollar signs flashing before her eyes. "*Very* nice…"

I slid my shoes on, grabbed my purse, and came down before she said or did anything else to embarrass me. Jonathan rose from his seat on the sofa, grinning appreciatively at the way I looked in my white and yellow sun dress.

"We have to go, mom!"

I grabbed Jonathan's hand and pulled him towards door, piercing my mother with invisible daggers on my way out.

"It was nice meeting you, Marjorie."

"My husband and I would love to have you over for drinks one day."

"I'll be sure to take you up on that."

"Pick your poison," mom dared.

"Brandy. *Old*."

Jonathan was just trying to be nice, but he was growing on me, slowly but surely.

"Take care of my baby, and Victoria? Good luck at your appointment."

I was going to need a lot more than luck. I felt guilty, withholding my suspicions from Marjorie.

My plan was to move out of the house before I told anyone about the pregnancy, and even then, I'd still be terrified to tell them what was going on.

"Nice lady," Jonathan said, on the way to the car. "I can see where you get your good looks."

I opened the car door and got in.

We soon made our way to Dr. Michaels' downtown family clinic. En route, Jonathan flipped through CDs and talked on the phone as I sat beside him, biting my fingernails down to the nub.

"Why don't you use the mp3 input? Jeesh. I'd think you, of all people, would be hip to the latest in auto technology."

He smiled, clasping a hand over mine. "Play whatever you want, I have a conference call."

He gestured towards the cell phone in his other hand. I turned the music off and took it away. He looked at me like I'd lost my mind.

"What in the hell are you doing? This is important, Tai, I have to take this." He sounded irritated.

"I'm saving our lives…" I chided.

I pressed the speaker button and attached the cell phone to Jonathan's dash. I wasn't about to end up in another car accident. I cared about Jonathan and didn't want either of us to get hurt, especially the baby. I could already feel its presence, its tiny being, coming to life inside of me.

"You win," he said, throwing his hands up in defeat.

I lurched towards the steering wheels, in the brief second he'd let go. Jonathan smirked at my skittishness.

Not long after, we arrived at the clinic. Jonathan waited outside in the car, still on a conference call as I went in. I was relieved as I wasn't exactly sure how I'd break the news to my new boss even *if*, he was slightly more than that.

The young blond nursing assistant at the check in station took my name and told me to fill out a form for my physical. I sat down, awkwardly placing the clipboard on my knees as I tried to write, waiting for someone to come out and call my name.

A few minutes later Dr. Michaels appeared. He scanned the waiting room, eyes locking on mine when he recognized my face.

"Victoria?"

I stood and he waved me over.

"How's everything?" he asked, in a friendly but officious tone.

"Fine, I guess."

I didn't even sound convincing to myself. I

thought I was going to faint I was so scared. Dr. Michaels was taking me to the scariest place in the whole building…the lab for a round of blood work.

"I'm nervous," I finally admitted, chewing my bottom lip.

"There's nothing to worry about. I'm sure everything will be alright," Dr. Michaels replied, pushing the elevator button.

The doors opened to a sterile white lab room where technicians and phlebotomists roamed around in scary white coats.

An older woman with a cart topped with vials, syringes, and tubes of varying sizes parked in front of me after I sat down.

"Ah! Miss Lawford I presume? Nice to meet you, my name is Lynn and I'll be taking your blood. Have you had your physical yet?"

"I thought I'd get Victoria's blood work taken care of, first. The test results should be in the system after the exam. Is that alright with you?"

"I'm just ready to get it over with," I sighed.

Dr. Michaels gave the woman a chart.

"What are we testing for?" I asked.

"Diabetes, inflammation, pregnancy, precancerous cells. Anything else on your mind, today?"

I looked down. Lynn had already pierced my skin, skillfully drawing three vials of blood.

"Not so bad, is it?"

I shook my head.

"All set?" Dr. Michaels asked.

Lynn unsnapped the latex strip from my upper arm and took her gloves off. Six vials of my blood were placed in a container on the inside of her cart. I felt faint just looking at it.

"All done!" the woman smiled.

I followed Dr. Michaels back to the elevator. We went to his office, on the second floor of the six story high medical building. He poured a blob of sanitizer in his hands, then opened the cabinet and gave me a plastic bag with a paper gown inside.

"Get undressed and put this on. I'll be back in a few minutes."

He left the room and I got undressed, leaving only my underwear and brassiere in place under the crepe paper gown. My entire backside was exposed in the horrendous suit. A few minutes later, Dr. Michaels tapped on the door and walked in.

"I read your chart, looks like you're having problems with indigestion…or maybe severe abdominal pains? How long has this been going on?"

"About two weeks now."

"Lay down please."

He gestured towards the examination table, pulling a tray from the bottom to support my legs.

"May I?" he asked, lifting the crepe paper gown.

I nodded and Dr. Michaels pressed the top of my stomach.

"You're not ticklish, are you?"

I grinned, though uncomfortably as he pressed my stomach all the way down to the lower part of my swollen pelvis.

"Ah!" he exclaimed, a cheerful gleam in his hazel-eyed gaze. "I think I have an answer for you."

"What is it?" I asked, half-sitting up.

"Congratulations…you're pregnant."

How could confirmation of such a beautiful thing engender so many emotions? I felt excited, scared, and alone all at the same time. If only O were here…I'd tell him he was going to be a father. The thought made me sigh.

"Are you okay?" Dr. Michaels asked.

"Are you sure—I mean, about the baby?"

"An enlarged or firm uterus is usually an indicator. You're far enough along to detect pregnancy."

"Do you know how many weeks?"

He pressed my uterus with the top of his fingers.

"Based on the size of your uterus, I'd guess about five or six weeks? I'll be back with results from your blood test. That should give us some answers."

Dr. Michaels opened the door just as Jonathan

was on the other side, about to knock. I pulled the crepe paper gown over my belly.

"Congratulations," the doctor smiled, slapping him on the shoulder as he walked in.

Jonathan closed the door behind him, shrugging like he was confused.

"What was that about?"

"I'm pregnant."

Jonathan stumbled back like he'd been shot.

"Wow!"

Then popped a toothpick in his mouth and sat on the edge of the examination table, swinging his legs.

"Your first love?"

"Who else?

He nodded, understanding.

"Do I still have a job?"

"Of course."

I sighed with great relief! He jumped down, pacing the white tiled floor.

"Have you told him yet?"

It was none of Jonathan's business, but he seemed so genuinely concerned it was hard to refuse the man an answer.

"If I knew where to find him…"

"What do you mean?"

"He's gone and he's not coming back. I told you our relationship was complicated."

"What a fool."

Jonathan crouched beside the examination table and kissed the back of my hand.

"You have my support. Anything you need… okay?"

"You're a good friend," I sighed, tears pricking the corners of my eyes.

"Well…" he said, caressing the back of my hand. "I hope to be more than that…someday."

Chapter Eleven

The sheer number of intellectuals at Senator Grayson's dinner party was enough to make me feel like I had a 2nd grade reading level. Conversations were casual enough, though layered with curious questions about what I did for a living and what my parents do, as if both were one in the same. I was out of my depth, like an ant swimming across the Atlantic Ocean as I intermingled among hard-boiled journalists and stiff-lipped wealthy elite, pretending I belonged. The room smelled of old money and crusty Ivy League college degrees.

I was the new political analyst for the Journal and only a few weeks in, but I didn't know who half of these people were. Why in the hell did Jonathan hire me, of all people? Politics was opposite of anything I'd ever been passionate about. In fact, it was the antidote to passion to anyone who wasn't a blustering ambitious prig like the ones sucking the life out of the room like a coven of vampires. I offered to bring a notepad to help keep track of everyone I met, but Jonathan said I had to train myself to remember names, faces, and details. Anything less, was dangerous. Plus, I'd end up looking like a neophyte, walking around with a pen and pad in my hands.

We tried to look officious as we strolled around, but ended up looking and feeling like were on yet another date. Jonathan and I giggled like a couple of teenagers as he whispered names and juicy tidbits about everyone we met. Details so comical, it was hard to greet them with a straight face.

He eventually introduced me to host of the party, Senator Grayson—a man whose ice cold handshake was as chilly as his grin. The attendees of his party were an equally cadaverous crowd of hoity-toity know nothings, all bent on deciding the lives of future generations like it was their God given duty. UGH! Words could not describe how much I hated politics. Others were just trying to get in where they fit in. Politicians of varying aspirations touched elbows with political adversaries, though smiling even as they conjured up ways to destroy each other professionally. Every step-every word, was a potential landmine and I was as good as dust.

I vetted the room…full of elected officials and their perfect-do wives all dressed to the nines for the social pages…on the other end of the spectrum, were my plainly suited my comrades, some dressed down in camouflage khakis, safari vests, and stealth reporter handbags like they'd just left the weeks-long trenches of Afghanistan- these were the younger guys, the over-important sods that they were.

My ever-growing relationship with Jonathan left me pondering what might well become a life of superficiality among these people, and it made me long for the quiet cove of love I had with O.

"Ask him about the new energy bill," Jonathan whispered, nudging my arm.

Senator Grayson had turned to speak to one of his assistants. They interrupted the man every other minute when they weren't waiting on him hand and foot.

"Wh-what? I can't, I'm not ready. What am I supposed to say?"

Jonathan nudged me again and my eyes shot to the floor. The Senator turned with a smile, to see what the commotion was about.

"I, ur, was just wondering, Senator, what your plans are for the new energy bill?"

I looked up, finally meeting a set of cool blue eyes. The man smiled, then quietly chuckled, shaking his head at Jonathan. "Shame on you, throwing this poor little girl to the wolves."

He offered me a gentle smile.

Jonathan tucked a hand into one of his pockets as the Senator gripped him by the elbow and swept him away to their little boy's club, a corner where the men talked shop and the perfect-do political wives sat on the sidelines to watch. The slight stung me so, that I grabbed my purse and marched outside to the patio, huffing away in anger, where Jonathan found me a few minutes later.

"What's wrong?" he asked, blinking like he was confused. "I've been looking all over the place for you!"

"I refuse to be condescended, Jonathan! How could you let him patronize me like that? I was so embarrassed."

I spoke in an angry but hushed voice. Jonathan sighed, shaking his head like I misunderstood.

"You have no relationship with this man, what was I supposed to say?"

"Then why did you tell me to ask him about the energy bill?"

"To open the conversation, Tai. Maybe if you asked with a little more confidence, he would have given you something. You have to get in there girl, guns blazing."

His hands settled on my shoulders, squeezing.

"Listen," he said, fingers gripping my upper arms. "I like having you around. The past few weeks have been…" he stopped, as if biting down on his emotions. "Just don't quit on me, Tai. Give it some time. Okay?"

"I'm not quitting my job," I sighed, trying to understand what he was trying to tell me. "Just because I'm mad, doesn't mean I'm cleaning my desk out tomorrow."

"I wasn't talking about work."

My arms dropped to my sides, mouth partly open as I fished around for a response. Jonathan looked around to see if anyone was looking then pulled me away from the patio to a secluded path in the Senator's rose garden, his hand gripping my wrist.

I spun out of his grasp, eyes gazing into desirous brown orbs. "What are you talking about?"

"*Us*," he said, with some urgency. "I want us, to be partners. Not just in work, but in life."

I stifled a giggle, what on earth was he on about?

"Please, Jonathan, spit it out already!"

We'd gotten as close as close could be in the past few weeks, sharing a kiss now and then, a meal, a trip or two for work related getaways. But I'd always sensed that these were only excuses to spend time alone, away from the prying eyes of our colleagues. People who watched, sensed our chemistry and growing affection.

Jonathan tipped my chin with the top of his index finger, tilting my face towards his to plant a kiss on my lips.

"Why are you doing this to yourself, Jonathan?

You know the situation I'm in."

"I don't care," he said, tenderly brushing hair away from my forehead. "We're perfect for each other. I'll do anything for you. You know that."

And indeed he had. He even spared me the trouble of living with my parents, helping me find a new apartment. I moved in two weeks after Dr. Michaels gave me the news. At my own apartment, I could at least deal with the first trimester of my pregnancy in private. It would only have been a matter of time before my parents put two and two together and realized I was suffering from morning sickness and not an extended bout of the stomach flu. Jonathan helped with the first month's rent, and I managed to float the second month on my own. I was moving into my second trimester and was already showing a tiny bump at 3 ½ months.

Jonathan went into his pocket, producing a small velvety navy blue box. He popped it open stretching his arm out towards me, a beautiful heart shaped diamond on display. I moved back like he was offering a pox infected blanket.

"Jonathan, please…I-I can't."

His face twisted like he was in pain.

"Why not?"

"Because I'm pregnant with another man's child!" I yelled. "I need closure. I can't do this to you…"

"Give him a call. Tell him it's over."

"I can't!"

"Why not?" he asked, face growing angrier by the second. *"Is he married?"*

I wondered if this is what he'd been thinking all along. I slowly met Jonathan's eyes, nodding my head. I couldn't tell him the truth…which is that I had been in an affair with the subject of one of my articles…that I loved *him* despite abandoning me and our unborn baby. And yet, I cared so much for Jonathan. I was afraid. I was certain his love for me would die a horrible fate if I told him anything about O.

"I knew it!" Jonathan said, pacing the secluded cobbled path. He grabbed my shoulders again, drawing me close to his chest. "You feel *something* for me, too. I know you do. Promise me you'll think about it, okay?"

He kissed my forehead. I grabbed his hand, and pressed it against my cheek, holding its warmth against my face. "Do you love me?" I asked, looking into his eyes.

"Of course I do! You're not only beautiful but you have a good heart. You're smart and passionate, a man would have to be crazy to leave you. What's wrong with this guy? I want you heart and soul. He had you, but *threw* you away. Now I can't have you because of him."

"I'm sorry…"

Tears stained the side of Jonathan's hand. He was right. I gave my heart to O and he threw it away. Whether he knew about our baby or not. He would have known if not for running away when things got tough. Jonathan was there for me through and through. I cared about Jonathan. Dare I say it, even loved him, even if I'll never love him as much as I loved O. I wasn't sure I knew how to love anyone with all of my heart again.

"I'm scared," I whispered, throwing myself into Jonathan's arms.

"Have I done anything to disappoint you, Tai?" His tone was confrontational.

"Of course, not! You've been a prince," I said, stroking the side of his face.

Jonathan took the ring out of its box and slid it on my finger. It twinkled against my skin like a star on the darkest of nights, even with the moon basking us in its luminous glow. ♥

Chapter Twelve

The engagement party was at my parent's house a week later. We invited a few our closest friends and family members, as if their enthusiasm and support confirmed in our minds that we were doing the right thing. Dana was there with her hot fireman boyfriend, Daniel. Jonathan's brother Carmichael and their sister Emily showed up, too.

I wore a baggy cream colored chiffon blouse and loose fitting pants. I avoided alcohol, though careful not to raise suspicions when I declined the margaritas my mother made for us.

But I was tired of hiding the pregnancy, and they were going to find out eventually. What should I do? Tell them when I was already six months along? All of a sudden I was compelled to tell everyone the truth…before I lost the courage.

"I'm pregnant," I blurted out, as mother served hors d'oeuvre to the room. She looked up at me, completely slack jawed.

"Victoria, what are you talking about?"

"I said I'm pregnant," I answered, a confrontational tone to my voice.

"*We're* pregnant," Jonathan continued.

Mom and dad sat on the sofa staring at me and Jonathan like they were waiting for the punch line of a joke.

"How long have you known?" my father asked.

"I'm 3 ½ months," I answered. "I moved out and got my own apartment to prove I could handle the responsibility."

Father shifted, uncomfortably, stabbing Jonathan with a sour look.

"I'm not happy about the sneaky way the two of you went about it. But you're an adult, Tai. What am I supposed to say?"

"I don't know, dad…"

I sat next to father and gave him hug. "Thanks, Dad, I knew you'd understand," I whispered.

"Well, I guess another round of congratulations is in order," Dana said, raising her glass. Emily and Carmichael joined in on the celebratory gesture, offering their brother pats on the back. It all felt so duplicitous.

I looked for reassurance in my mother's eyes, but she stormed out of the room.

I released my father and followed mother into the kitchen where she dumped ice into a blender for margaritas, huffing with anger.

"I'd offer you a drink," she said, a chill in her voice, "but you're in a delicate way so…"

I opened my mouth to speak but she pressed a button, filling the room with noise. I waited until the blender stopped.

"I'm sorry, mom, we wanted to tell you but…"

She turned and glared at me. "No more lies, Victoria. That's not that man's child and you know it."

She gestured angrily towards living room where Jonathan sat.

"How could you do this to yourself?"

"I'm sorry mom, it's not like I planned it."

"Your life is *messy* and you better fix it. O needs to do the honorable thing and take care of his kid. It's not right to dump the responsibility on another man, and I won't stand for it."

"Okay mom, I'll take care of it," I sighed.

"You better."

Marjorie brushed past me and stormed out of the kitchen. I followed her into the living room, eyes brimming with tears. Jonathan left his seat on the sofa and grabbed my hand.

"Have you set a date?" my father asked.

"Next month. I'll make arrangements," Jonathan said. "Something intimate, if that's okay?"

I watched mom through a mirror hanging on our wall as she mixed her drink, refusing to look at either of us as she guzzled it down.

"Marjorie and I put money away for Tai. We were hoping for a big wedding."

Like the one I planned with Everett before he died.

Mom rolled her eyes, like paying for our wedding was the last thing she wanted to hear.

"It's a gunshot wedding, Harold. Leave it alone. Buy her some baby clothes, instead."

"Not now, we'll talk about it later," my father advised.

"That's right, we should be celebrating," Dana replied, doing her best to sound cheerful.

I sighed. The party was turning into a disaster.

"Maybe Victoria and I should call it a night," Jonathan offered, sensing the dour change in mood.

"What about dinner?" his sister Emily, asked.

"We'll do it some other time," he replied. "If that's okay with Mr. And Mrs. Lawford?"

Mom gave him a sarcastic look.

"Fine by us," my father replied. "We'll do it another night, maybe at the local tavern over a couple of beers. Not that Tai can drink…"

"I don't need a drink, a tavern is fine, dad."

"Good. Then it's settled."

"There's one more thing," Jonathan said.

"What now?" Mother replied.

"Victoria and I were talking about the wedding. We're thinking of doing it next month, before her pregnancy really begins to show," he smiled. "She wants to fit into her wedding dress. I talked to the pastor of my church, he agreed to officiate."

"Then I guess everything *is* settled," my father answered.

"We could use some help with decorations. Any volunteers?" Jonathan said.

"I can help," Dana replied. "Mrs. Lawford?" Dana nudged my mother with her elbow.

"Come on, you know you wanna…"

Mom looked up from the margarita she drank. "Well…I guess I can do something. Have you decided on what color you're going to wear?"

"Pink, I guess..."

"Is it because you're having a girl? Be careful…a daughter will one day break your heart," mother sobbed.

Father left his seat on the sofa and wrapped his arms around her shoulders. It dawned on me at that moment, that mom was not only mad about the situation with O, but was probably feeling left out.

That night, Jonathan and I went back to my apartment, a small two bedroom…one for me, the other for the baby.

"That didn't go as bad as I thought it would."

"She's mad because we planned the wedding and did everything without her. She doesn't know where to fit in."

"She'll come around."

"You told everyone that you were the father. You sure that's a good idea?"

"We're getting married and I'm raising this kid as my own, so why shouldn't I?"

"I don't want you to get hurt."

"Who's going to hurt me?" he asked, inching forward to take my hands into his own.

"Not me," I answered.

"Is that a promise?"

I nodded and Jonathan kissed me on the lips.

"Now that the secret's out, when are we going to do this moving in, thing?"

I withdrew my hand from his and tried to look busy, tidying up the room. Somewhere in my heart, I knew I wasn't ready to be with Jonathan or anyone else. My heart belonged to O. But Jonathan was perfect, and so very good to me that I couldn't bear to disappoint him.

"After the wedding, of course."

"What about your lease?"

"I'll sublet."

"Good."

Jonathan started towards the door. "Walk me out," he demanded.

I smiled, glowing as I followed him to the door. I stood on my tippy toes as he kissed me on the lips, whispering *"Goodnight."*

When he was finally gone, I turned the lights down and ran a bath. I was glad the pregnancy was out in the open now, even if I was keeping the real father a secret from everyone, including my fiancé.

I got undressed and wrapped a towel around my body, laughing quietly to myself at how it almost didn't fit. I sat on the edge of the tub and dipped my fingers in the water, testing the temperature, when all of a sudden, a figure appeared in the water's reflection.

"You can't marry him," a voice said.

I turned, to find Mihoko standing behind me.

Suddenly, her hand was reaching out, pushing me into the tub. I landed on my shoulder, the side of my face going into the water. I nearly lost my towel. I held it together with one of my hands, practically drowning. The last thing I wanted was that bitch to see me naked.

How she managed to get in my apartment was the last thing on my mind, it's what she had planned to do next that concerned me. I mounted a fight, pushing out of the water with enough force to knock her back.

"Get the hell out of my apartment!" I screamed, choking on the water that slipped into my mouth.

I looked at her clothes. They were soaking wet.

Mihoko produced a knife, and pointed it at my chest. "Get out of the tub, slut."

I stood with my back against the wall, water up to my knees. The bath was still running, about to overflow.

"What do you want, Mihoko?"

"I want my husband," she answered.

I shook my head. "I don't know what you're talking about."

"Shut---UP!" she screamed. "I'm sick of your lies!"

"What lies?" I pleaded. I don't know what you're talking about ..."

She pointed the knife at my throat.

"Stay here," she said, producing a bottle of liquid from out of her jacket pocket.

I watched as she squirted the contents all over the bathroom floor, backing into the hall onto the carpet.

"What are you doing?" I asked, though it was obvious what her intentions were.

"Yoshihiro is supposed to be my husband. But you ruined everything."

I stared at her tear-streaked face, stunned. The girl had gone completely mad. What was she talking about?

"B-but he's your brother..." I gasped.

"That's not true…" Mihoko shook her head. "I moved to America with Yoshihiro's family when I was a little girl, just after my parents died. My grandfather made an arrangement with the Otari family. Yoshihiro and I were supposed to get married to pay off his father's old gambling debt and you ruined it. His family will be in financial ruin because of you. He has refused to marry me. I don't have a family now, and it's your fault."

Mihoko pulled a box of matches from one of her pockets. I looked down as the bath began to overflow. Drops of blood trickled into the water from the side of my head. I could feel the rivulet of blood pouring down my face onto my lips and chin.

"Don't do this, Mihoko…" I pleaded.

I looked for a means of escape, but she blocked the only way out. I couldn't' take a chance, what if she poured the flammable liquid in her container directly on me? What about the baby?

"O and I are over, now. I'm getting married."

Mihoko laughed. "That sham of a marriage will never work, not if Yoshihiro has his way. He wanted to marry you."

The girl struck a match. I had to think of something…and fast.

"Why are you doing this, Mihoko? Because he's done protecting you, and covering your tracks?

Why would O want someone as crazy as you?"

Mihoko glared at me, the flame dwindling at her finger tips. I was starting to get dizzy from the loss of blood.

"The Nakoda the mafia arranged for you and O will allow you out of the agreement if one of you is no longer suitable. Is that what you're doing? You're not in love with Yoshihiro. You're in love with someone else, aren't you?

The look in her eyes softened. "How did you know," Mihoko asked, lips trembling…

'Because no one, would do this to the man she loved…you'd want him to be happy. You framed him for the arsons so the agreement can be broken and you can marry whoever you wanted. Yoshihiro took the blame, because he loved you, and thought he was protecting his sister. His parents never told him about his role in the arrangement."

A tear strolled down Mihoko's cheek. "It's not fair," she blurted, striking another match. "It's my life! I can't marry him…"

"You don't have to Mihoko, it's your choice, just say no!"

Mihoko shook her head.

"Everyone will think Yoshihiro killed you in a jealous rage. Bye, *bitch*!"

I touched the side of my face with trembling fingers as Mihoko hurled the match onto the carpeted floor. All of sudden a hand struck out, knocking her on the back of her head with my bronzed baseball trophy. I sunk into the bath, too weak to stand any longer. Relieved Mihoko had been stopped.

I looked up expecting to see Jonathan with the trophy in his hand, but it was O who stood before me. He reached into the bath and pulled me out, stepping over Mihoko as he carried me to the bedroom.

"I'll call the police," he whispered, gently setting me down.

He pressed a towel against the side of my head and I closed my eyes. The lump on the side of my head hurt like hell.

"Don't go to sleep," O demanded, shaking me awake.

But the temptation to rest was too great to resist. I closed my eyes again, knowing O would never leave my side, not until Mihoko had been put away for good.

When I awakened a spell later, Dana and O were next to the bed, a couple of police officers and an EMS crew standing behind them.

A medic peered into my eyes with a flashlight.

"It's okay, kiddo. She's on her way to the pokey," Dana said.

"We're taking you to the hospital," O continued,

concern edging his voice.

"I don't need a doctor, I'm fine," I answered, waving them off.

Dana sat on the edge of my bed. "You have to think of the baby now," she offered gently. "We need to make sure he's okay."

I shook my head. "She didn't touch me."

"Then where'd that lump on your temple come from? The medic said you might have a contusion."

I remembered falling into the tub. The details were starting to come back. O sat on the other side of the bed and held my hand. "I'm going with you," he said.

"You can't…" I whispered, trying to show some loyalty to Jonathan. "Dana, I need to call Jonathan to let him know I'm alright."

"Don't worry about him…I'll take care of it. You *and* Mr. Otari should get to the hospital to check on your baby."

O gripped my hand as the EMS team hauled me onto a stretcher and carried me to the ambulance. He rode all the way to the hospital, staying by my side the entire time.

I wondered if Jonathan would show up. What will happen then? Would I have to make a choice right there on the spot?

O disappeared, and Jonathan had done everything a man could possibly do to win my heart. To leave him now would be to betray him most.

****

O slept in the chair next to my bed and was the first thing I saw when I opened my eyes the next day. I gazed longingly at his face as he slept. As if sensing that I was awake, he opened his eyes.

"I talked to the doctor. Our baby is fine," he said, careful to use the word *"our."*

He closed the space between the hospital bed and the chair, gripping my hand.

"What do we do now?" I asked.

O smiled. "Get married. Nothing or no one can stand in our way, now."

I wanted to believe him, but there were too many unanswered questions.

"But I'm already engaged," I answered.

O got out of the chair and stood next to my bed, holding both of my hands. "You don't love him, Victoria…you love *me*--and I'm in love with you," he pleaded.

"You didn't tell me about your engagement to Mihoko!"

O sighed. "I didn't know I was part of the arrangement until I was arrested for the fire at the Pancake House. My parents visited me in jail that

212

night and begged me not to expose her. They said we had to marry to pay off an old gambling debt to some mafia outfit in Japan. They would also inherit the money Mihoko's parents left as a dowry. They said we needed the money to save the restaurant. But I refused…and now my parents have disowned me…even though I paid their debt to the IRS to save the restaurant from foreclosure."

"Why would they disown you after everything you've done?"

"Because I disobeyed. Our culture is different, Victoria. I sacrificed everything to be with you."

"O, you shouldn't have done that. I would never ask you to."

"I would do it all over again to be with you. We deserve to be happy. Why should I spend the rest of my life paying for *their* mistakes?"

"What about the mafia?" I asked, worried.

"This is America," O smiled. "It was a low-level Japanese outfit *in* Japan. We're safe. They have no power, here."

He caressed my face. I sighed, content with his answer…*for now*.

"What about Mihoko? How did you know where to find us?"

"Simple. I knew it was only a matter of time before she went after you and your family. Gangsters and their children have an unsavory way of dealing with people. I've been following her for weeks, now. I stayed away to protect you. I only recently learned that Mihoko wasn't my biological sister…if I had known sooner, and made my intentions to be with you clear to my parents, the situation might have been avoided. I feel sorry for Mihoko, none of this was our fault, and now her life is over."

"A man died, O. She made a choice. *She tried to kill me and my baby!*"

O looked up at the monitor over my bed. Wires had been attached to my stomach to detect the baby's heartbeat, which was steady enough, though rising and falling occasionally.

He watched the heart rate for a moment then said, "You have to take it easy, Victoria."

"What about the baby?" I asked, wondering how he knew.

"I figured it out when I saw you at the apartment."

"And the father?"

"Who else could it be?" he asked…though it was more of a declaration, than a question.

"I thought I would never see you again. I feel terrible," I cried, wiping tears from my eyes. "I used Jonathan as a way out."

O shrugged.

"I honestly could care less. He knew the risks of

marrying a woman carrying another man's child. Besides…"

O went into his pocket, producing a ring with three stones. I remembered the diamonds in the shoebox I found in his closet that day.

O took the ring out of its box and slid it onto my finger. I made a fist, admiring the gift he had given me. O grabbed the remote on my bed and pressed the call button for the nurse. A minute later, someone knocked on the door.

For a moment, I fretted, wondering who was on the other side. Thankfully, the nurse walked in, the hospital's chaplain behind her.

"You summoned?" the man said.

O held my hand. "I asked the chaplain to marry us," he said.

He drew me into his arms and held tight.

"What about my parents?" I asked.

"They're in the waiting room. They'll be here in a few minutes," he answered.

All the worries of the world melted away. I kissed O on the lips for as long as I could. The door opened. Dana and my parents walked in.

"You're supposed to kiss *after* the vows," the chaplain explained.

Dana laughed.

"You're getting married in white!" my mother exclaimed, closing the door behind them. I wore a white hospital gown, surrounded by white bedding. Father gave me a bouquet of flowers from the hospital gift shop.

Mom took my hand, and sat on the other side of the bed. "Congratulations, sweetheart... This," she said, "feels right, to me."

"Shall we begin?" the chaplain asked.

"What about wedding bands?" my father inquired.

"Oh!" I exclaimed.

Dana went into her pocket, producing a pair of small brown rubber bands. "Don't ask why I carry these around. I have my reasons…" she said.

"Then let us begin," the chaplain continued.

"Two lives, so different, yet the same, prepare today to come together in holy matrimony for the purpose of sharing their lives as one. Lord bless this day, and the future of this blessed couple, as they unite forever in holy matrimony, Amen."

I gripped O's hand, unsure if I were actually awake or if it was all a dream. If it was, I would rather sleep forever than to live without him.

"Do you, uh…uh…umm…" The chaplain began. He looked around, somewhat flustered.

"I'm sorry, what is your name again?" The man asked.

I looked up at O and smiled.

"Yoshihiro Otari," he answered, smiling back.

"Do you, Yoshihiro Otari, take--"

"Victoria Taisha Lawford," I interrupted.

"Take Victoria Taisha Lawford as your lawfully wedded wife…" the man continued. "To have, and to hold, from this day forward…"

I didn't remember much about the wedding, as it all went by in a blur. I do remember when Yoshihiro uttered, "I will" -- as did I…becoming *Victoria Lawford Otari*, something I thought would never happen.

"You may kiss the bride," the chaplain commanded.

I looked at my father, who turned away, still yet unable to see me with a boy, even my own husband, and father of my unborn child.

"Mrs. Otari?" O whispered….

"Yes?"

One look into his eyes and I knew. Yoshihiro kissed me until I was *breathless*, promising…no matter what, never to disappear, again.

THE END.

<u>Page 221</u>
Sneak Peek, *Sixth Iteration* by E. Hughes

Again, My Love
Sequel to *Disappear, Love* coming soon

Betrayed by the cold, hardened nipples pushed through my wet t-shirt. I self-consciously wrapped my arms across my chest while moving my legs back and forth to keep warm as Randall emerged from the shadows.

"What are you doing here?" I asked.

"A sensor picked up activity on the tower and tripped the silent alarm before the power went out."

His eyes, sensuous and seductive in the dark focused intently on my face.

I shrugged. "Oh, well...it's just me."

He stepped into the light, his angular visage and muscular physique in full view. Corpulent drops of rain pelted his long sleeved shirt, soaking it through to bare skin. *I could drink him.*

"Everything's fine, but thank you," I continued.

Two steps across the balcony brought us face to face. The once stern features of a man who took almost everything too seriously, now sensuously playful, was smiling, now. His eyes were drinking *me*. I suddenly wished I wasn't standing there in my pink panties. I wrapped my arms even tighter and hoped he didn't look down.

"The tower is the highest point on the island for miles. It's not safe out here in a lightning storm."

"I know."

Trying a different tack, he gestured towards the stairs.

"Would you care to join me? *Inside*?"

Quivering, I shook my head and gazed outward towards the stormy terrain.

"I love storms," I offered.

I could feel the heat of his gaze tracing the outline of my face as I looked away.

"I know," Randall replied.

He took a small step forward, narrowing the space between us. Suddenly, our eyes were tidally locked. The smoldering intensity of his magnetic gaze held mine as an overpowering energy drew me to him. The corners of his mouth lifted into a barely perceptible smile. I couldn't remember Randall ever looking at me like that before. I couldn't remember him ever looking at me at all.